HARF
AND
GRACE

Written by John Chalmers
Illustrated by Sandra Marrs

Collins

Chapter 1

Harris and Grace lived with their parents at the edge of a large town. Today was the very first day of their summer holiday. It was only 8 o'clock and already you could feel the heat in the air. Their mum and dad had got up early to make their favourite breakfast: pancakes, with blueberries and raspberries too.

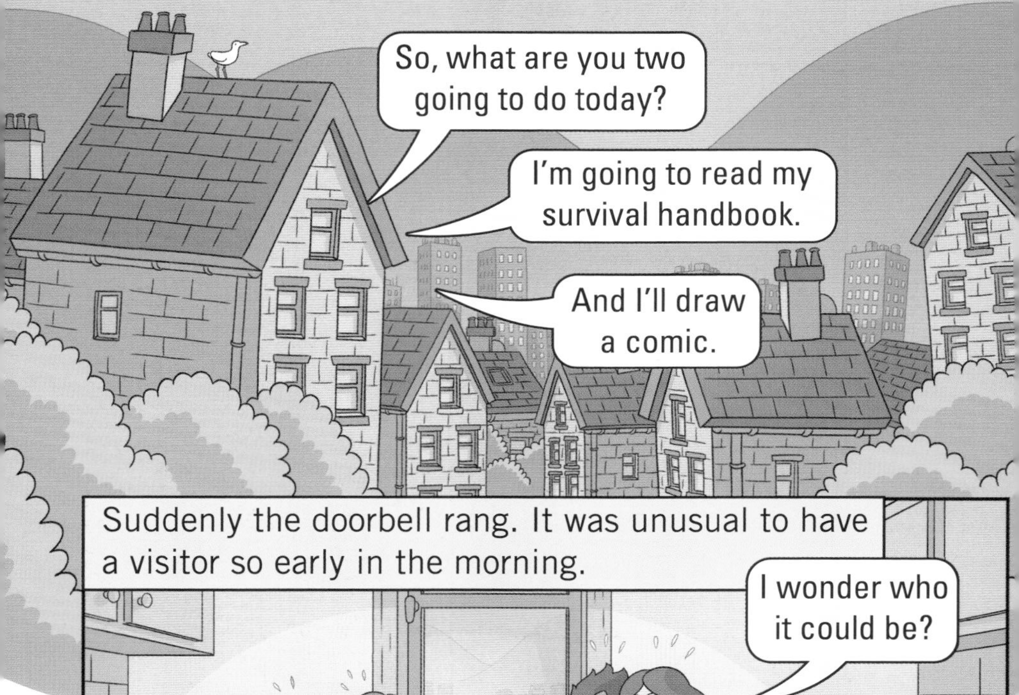
So, what are you two going to do today?
I'm going to read my survival handbook.
And I'll draw a comic.

Suddenly the doorbell rang. It was unusual to have a visitor so early in the morning.

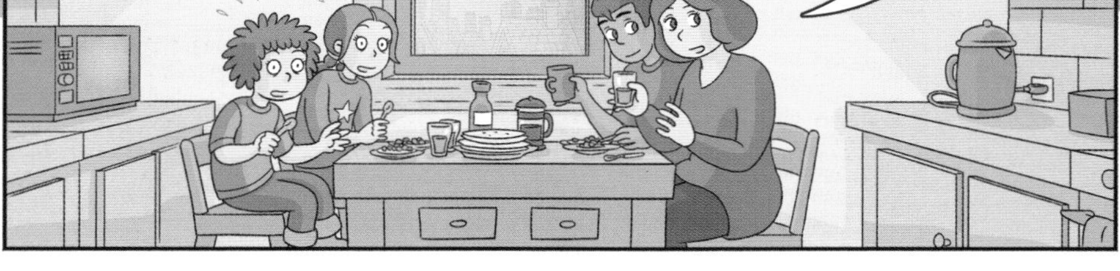
I wonder who it could be?

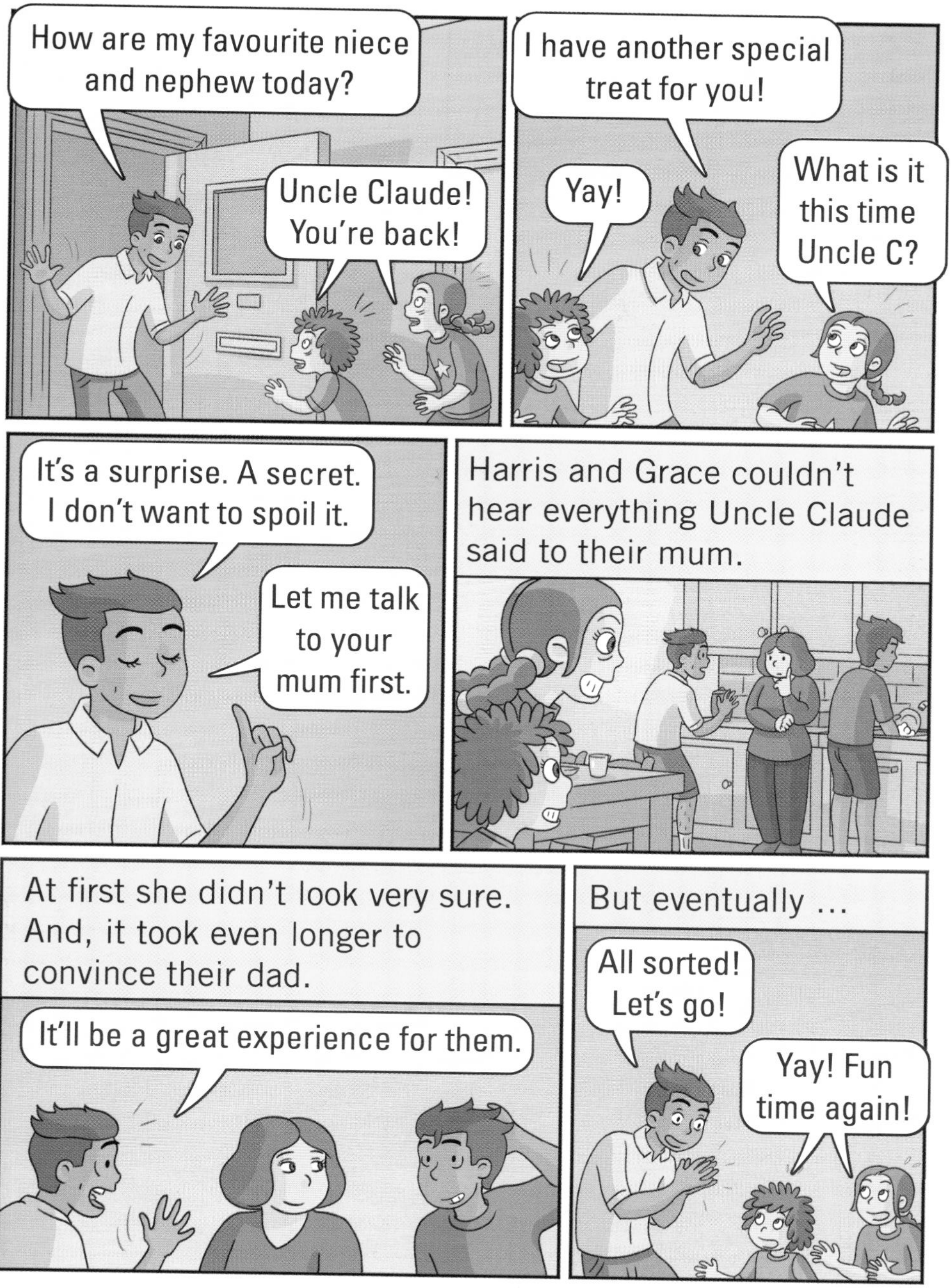
How are my favourite niece and nephew today?
Uncle Claude! You're back!
I have another special treat for you!
Yay!
What is it this time Uncle C?
It's a surprise. A secret. I don't want to spoil it.
Let me talk to your mum first.
Harris and Grace couldn't hear everything Uncle Claude said to their mum.
At first she didn't look very sure. And, it took even longer to convince their dad.
It'll be a great experience for them.
But eventually …
All sorted! Let's go!
Yay! Fun time again!

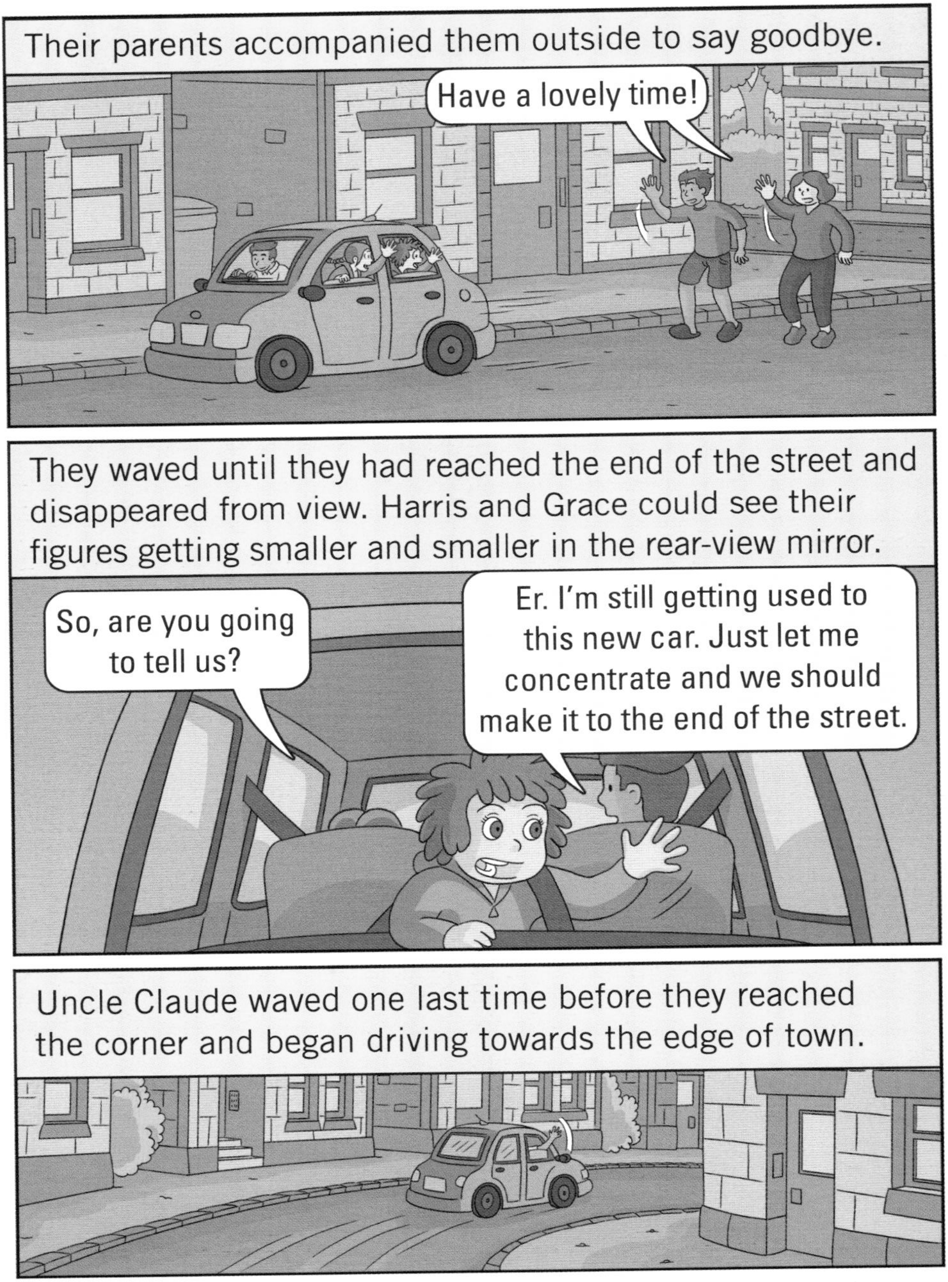
Their parents accompanied them outside to say goodbye.
Have a lovely time!
They waved until they had reached the end of the street and disappeared from view. Harris and Grace could see their figures getting smaller and smaller in the rear-view mirror.
So, are you going to tell us?
Er. I'm still getting used to this new car. Just let me concentrate and we should make it to the end of the street.
Uncle Claude waved one last time before they reached the corner and began driving towards the edge of town.

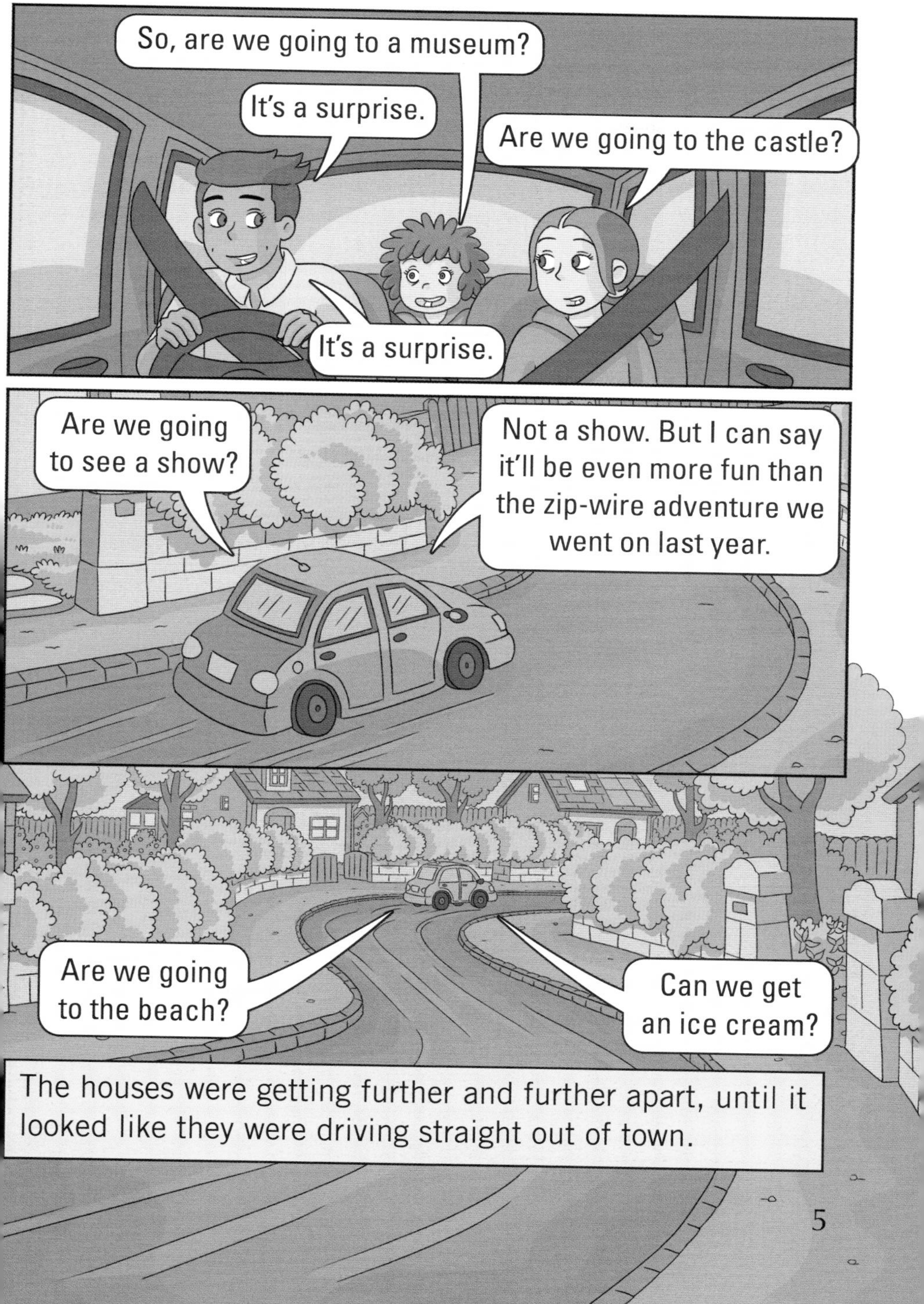
So, are we going to a museum?
It's a surprise.
Are we going to the castle?
It's a surprise.
Are we going to see a show?
Not a show. But I can say it'll be even more fun than the zip-wire adventure we went on last year.
Are we going to the beach?
Can we get an ice cream?
The houses were getting further and further apart, until it looked like they were driving straight out of town.

Chapter 2

After the town came the countryside. They drove through hills and wide-open green space. Brightly-coloured yellow fields and small farmhouses appeared occasionally at the side of the road. Uncle Claude wound his window down and inhaled with an exaggerated relish.

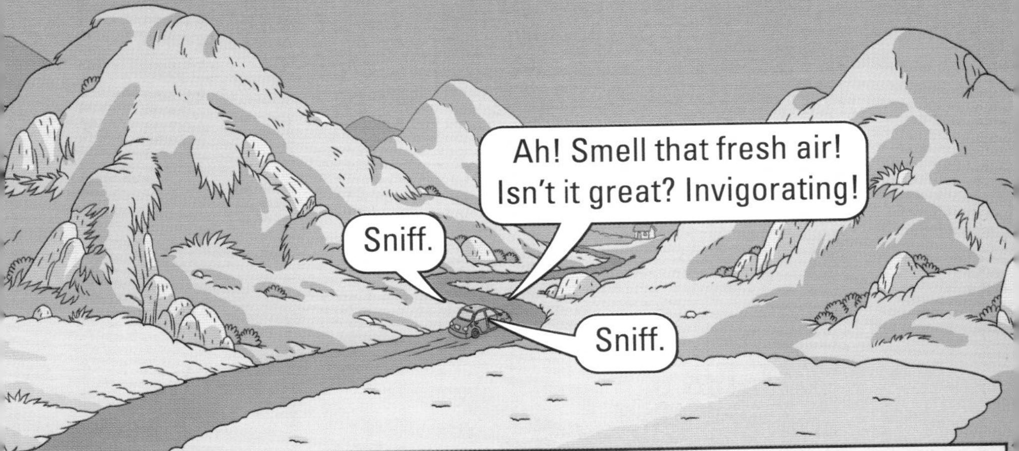
Ah! Smell that fresh air! Isn't it great? Invigorating!
Sniff.
Sniff.

They had been driving for at least an hour when they came to a small hamlet. Houses slept behind closed wooden shutters.

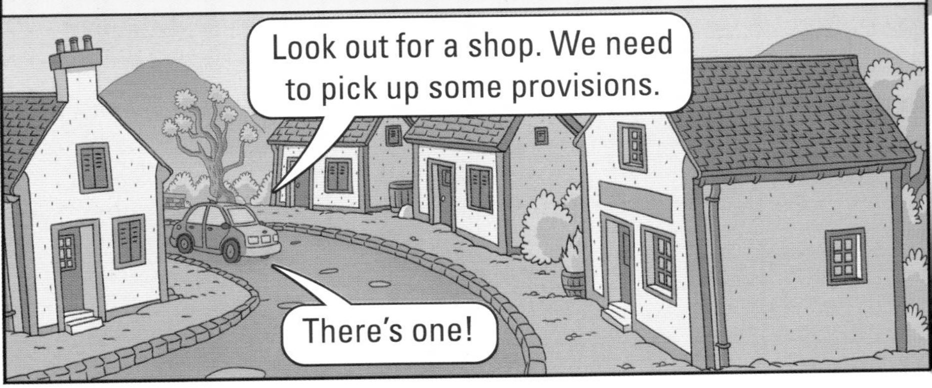
Look out for a shop. We need to pick up some provisions.
There's one!

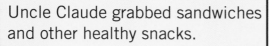

Uncle Claude grabbed sandwiches and other healthy snacks.

Let's see ... we'll need sandwiches for tonight. And cereal bars for breakfast.

You mean we're not going home tonight?

Nope.

I think I know where we're going.

Could you give us directions to the forest near the loch please?

You mean Loch Monaharr?

That's over by Frannoch Forest, aye.

Well I'll tell you: you'll no be wanting to go there.

Aye. Naw. Aye.

Haunted. So it be. Haunted. The loch.

Aye. Ghosts.

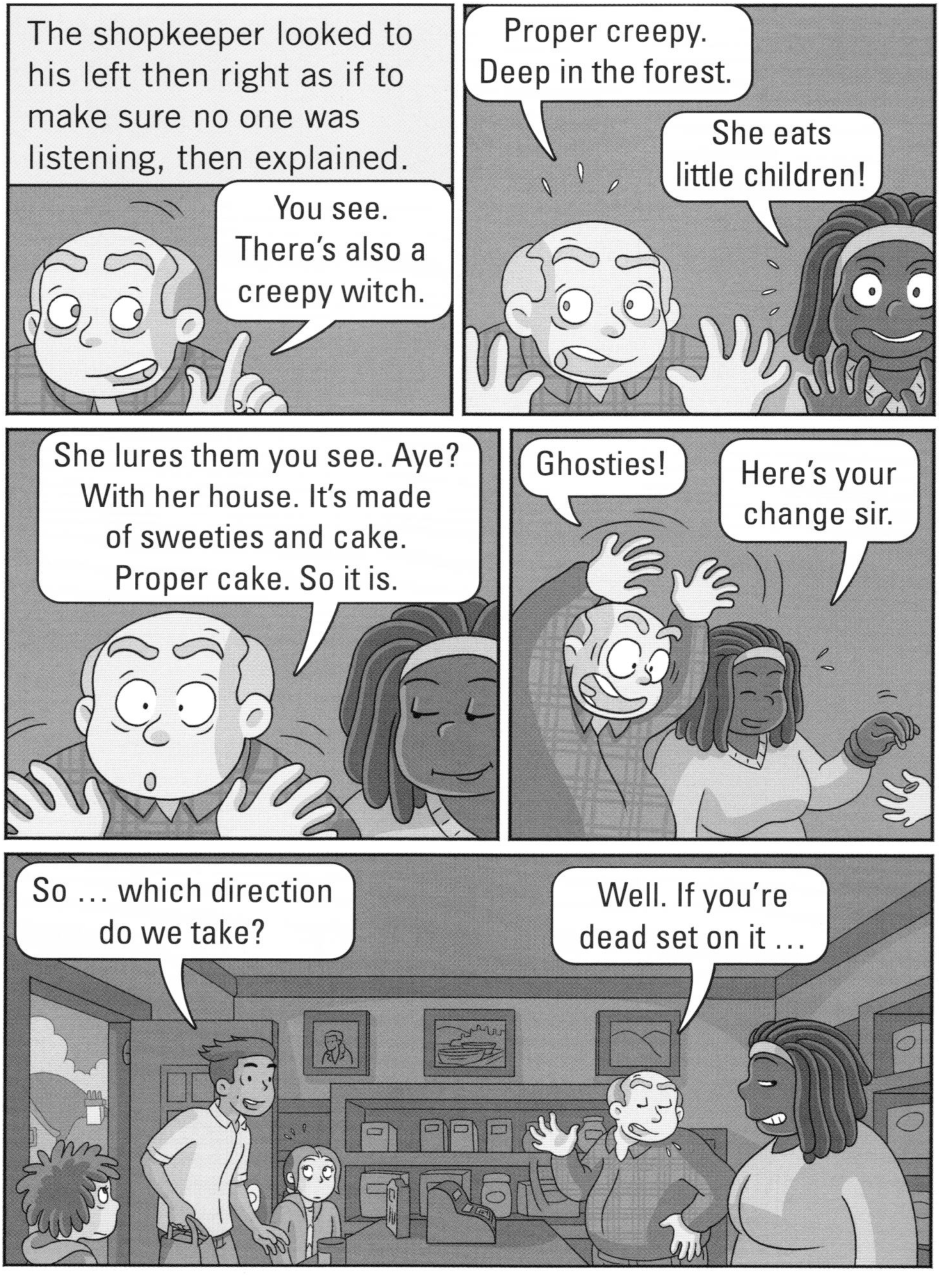

The shopkeeper looked to his left then right as if to make sure no one was listening, then explained.
You see. There's also a creepy witch.
Proper creepy. Deep in the forest.
She eats little children!
She lures them you see. Aye? With her house. It's made of sweeties and cake. Proper cake. So it is.
Ghosties!
Here's your change sir.
So … which direction do we take?
Well. If you're dead set on it …

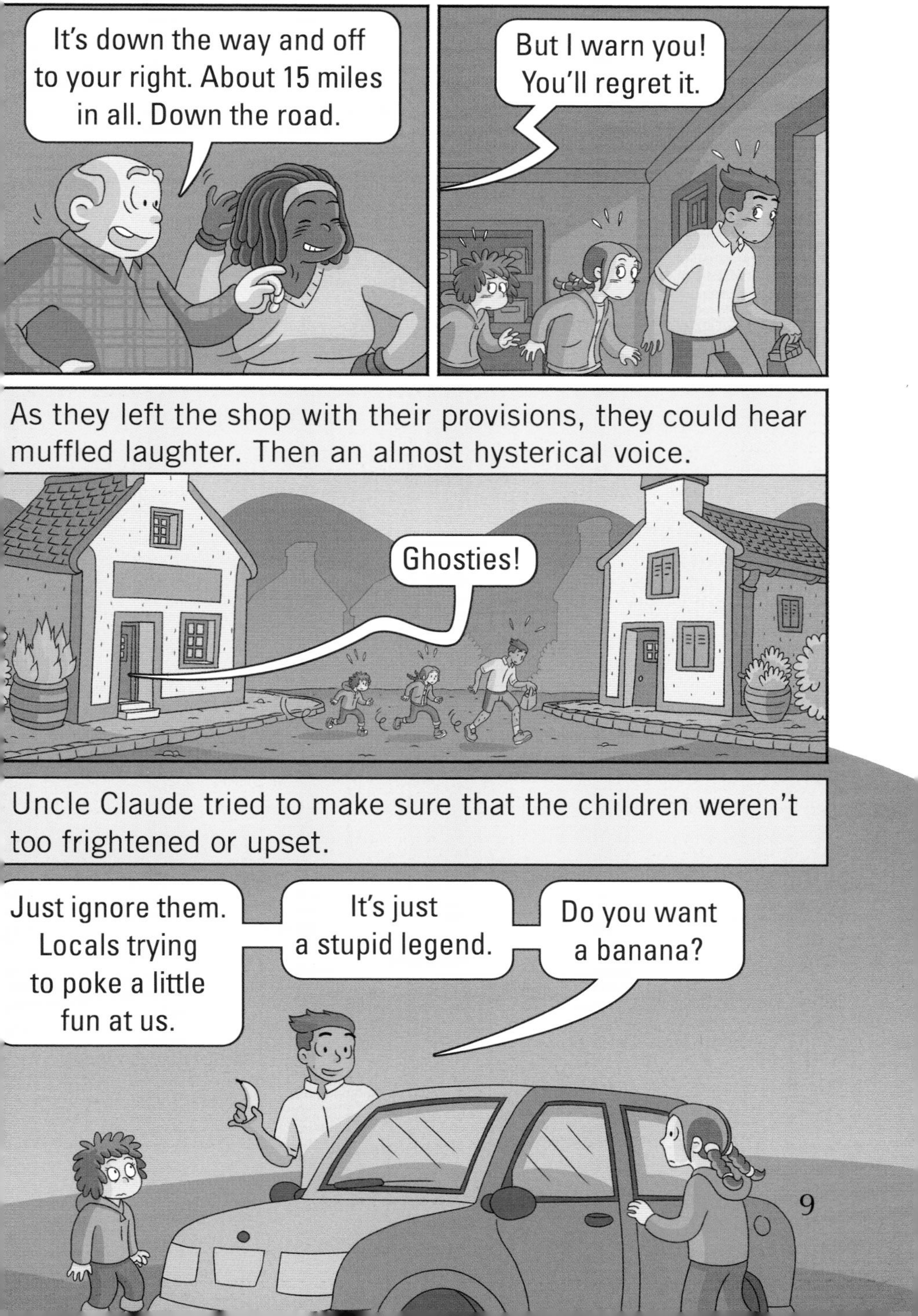
It's down the way and off to your right. About 15 miles in all. Down the road.
But I warn you! You'll regret it.
As they left the shop with their provisions, they could hear muffled laughter. Then an almost hysterical voice.
Ghosties!
Uncle Claude tried to make sure that the children weren't too frightened or upset.
Just ignore them. Locals trying to poke a little fun at us.
It's just a stupid legend.
Do you want a banana?

Chapter 3

No one had said a word since they left the hamlet.
And then Harris voiced what they had all been thinking.

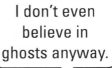

I don't even believe in ghosts anyway.

Yeah, me neither. Or witches.

Witches don't even exist. They were just women who were persecuted for being a bit different.

There were witch hunts in the Middle Ages and thousands of women were accused of witchcraft.

They put them in water and if they floated it meant they were a witch.

That's pretty gruesome.

Yeah and I'm quite sure men and children were accused too. Thankfully people are less superstitious now.

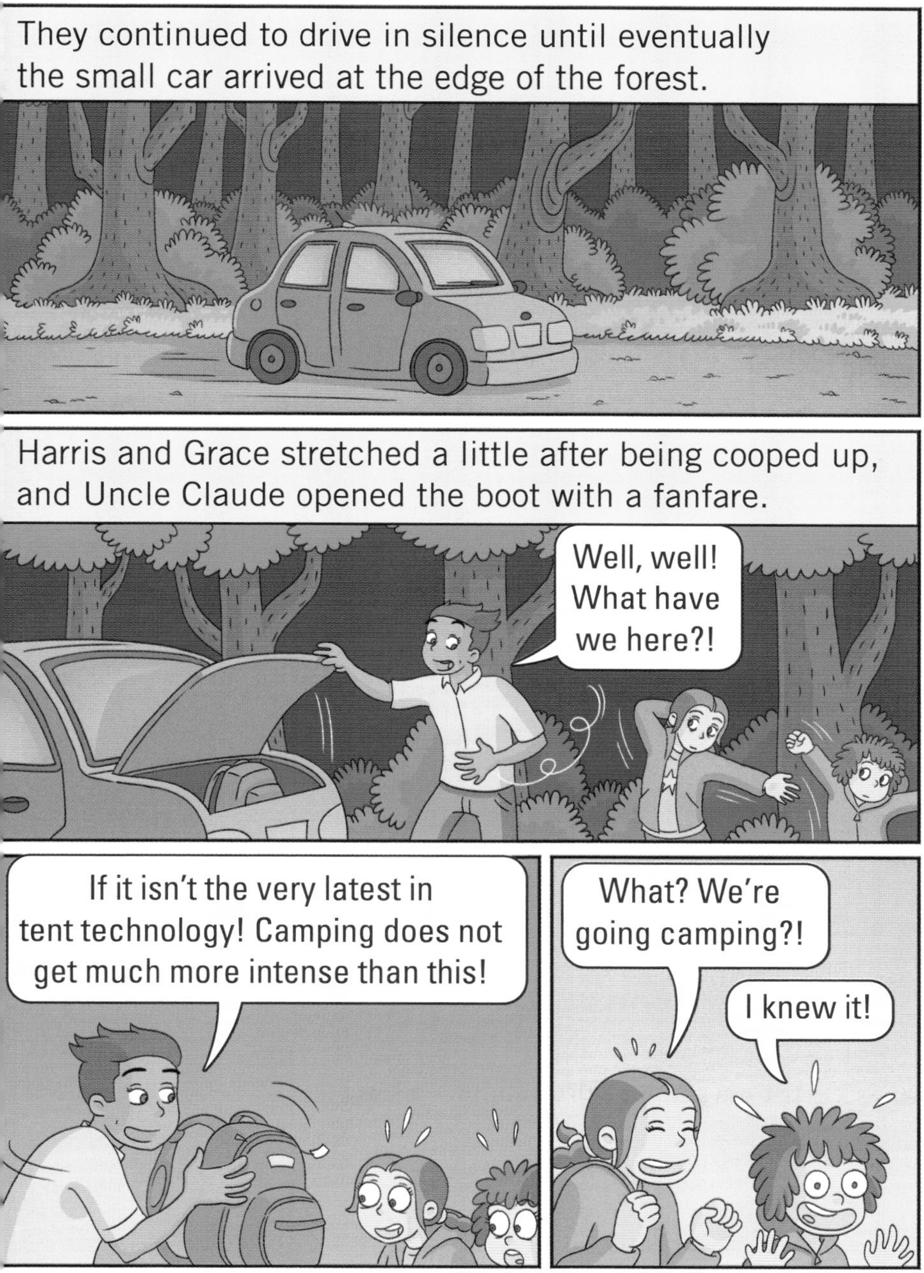
They continued to drive in silence until eventually the small car arrived at the edge of the forest.
Harris and Grace stretched a little after being cooped up, and Uncle Claude opened the boot with a fanfare.
Well, well! What have we here?!
If it isn't the very latest in tent technology! Camping does not get much more intense than this!
What? We're going camping?!
I knew it!

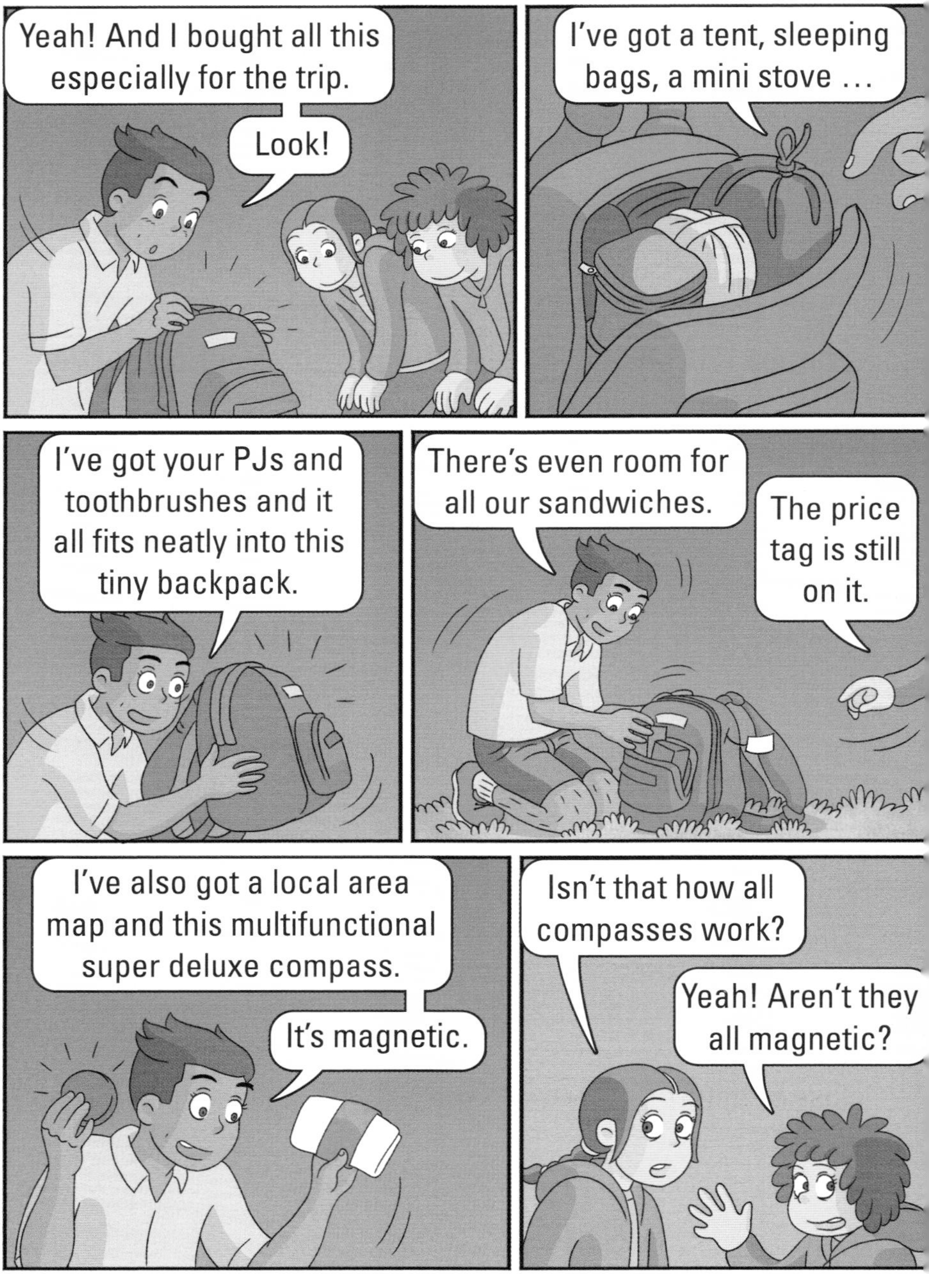
Yeah! And I bought all this especially for the trip.
Look!
I've got a tent, sleeping bags, a mini stove …
I've got your PJs and toothbrushes and it all fits neatly into this tiny backpack.
There's even room for all our sandwiches.
The price tag is still on it.
I've also got a local area map and this multifunctional super deluxe compass.
It's magnetic.
Isn't that how all compasses work?
Yeah! Aren't they all magnetic?

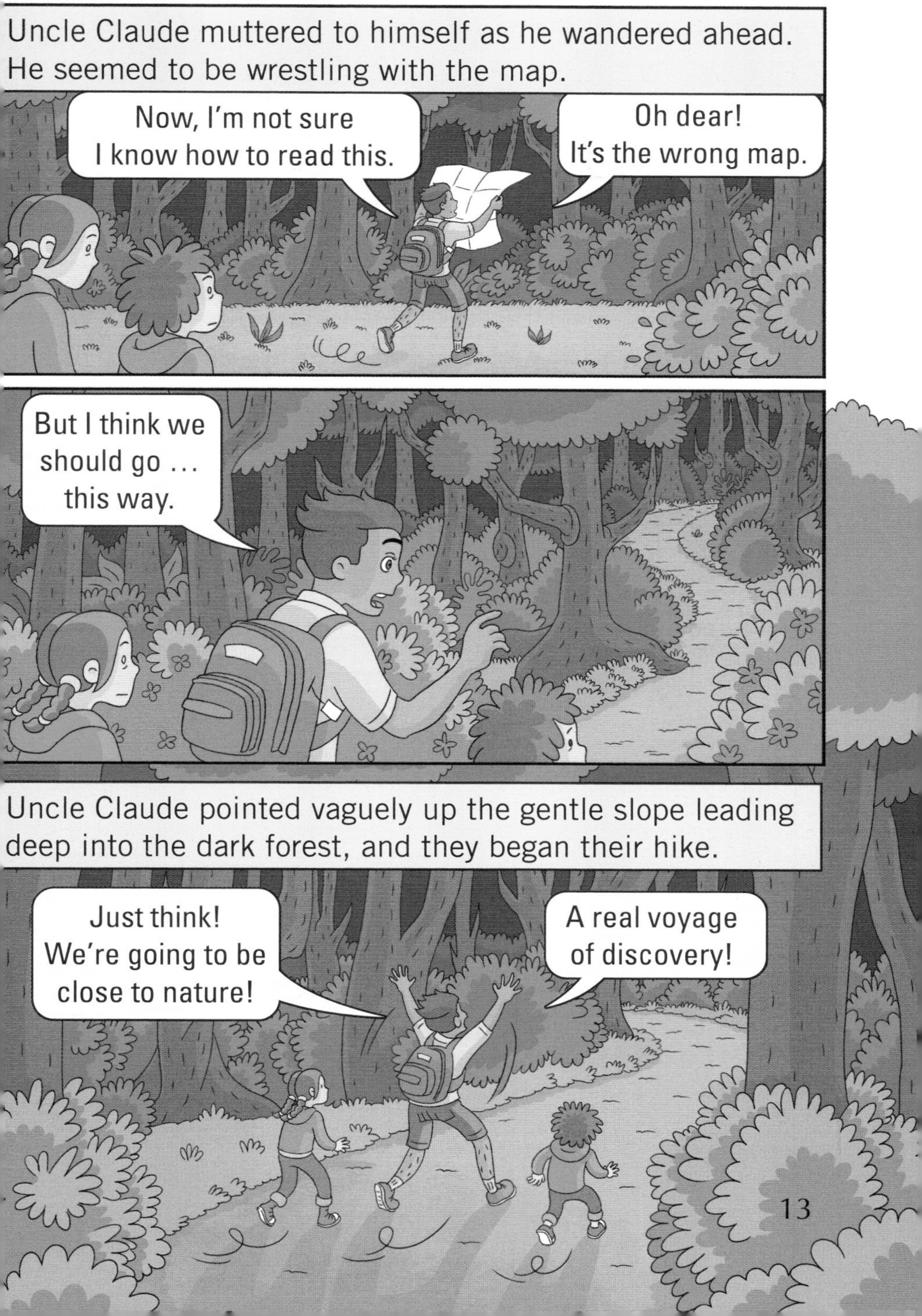
Uncle Claude muttered to himself as he wandered ahead. He seemed to be wrestling with the map.
Now, I'm not sure I know how to read this.
Oh dear! It's the wrong map.
But I think we should go … this way.
Uncle Claude pointed vaguely up the gentle slope leading deep into the dark forest, and they began their hike.
Just think! We're going to be close to nature!
A real voyage of discovery!

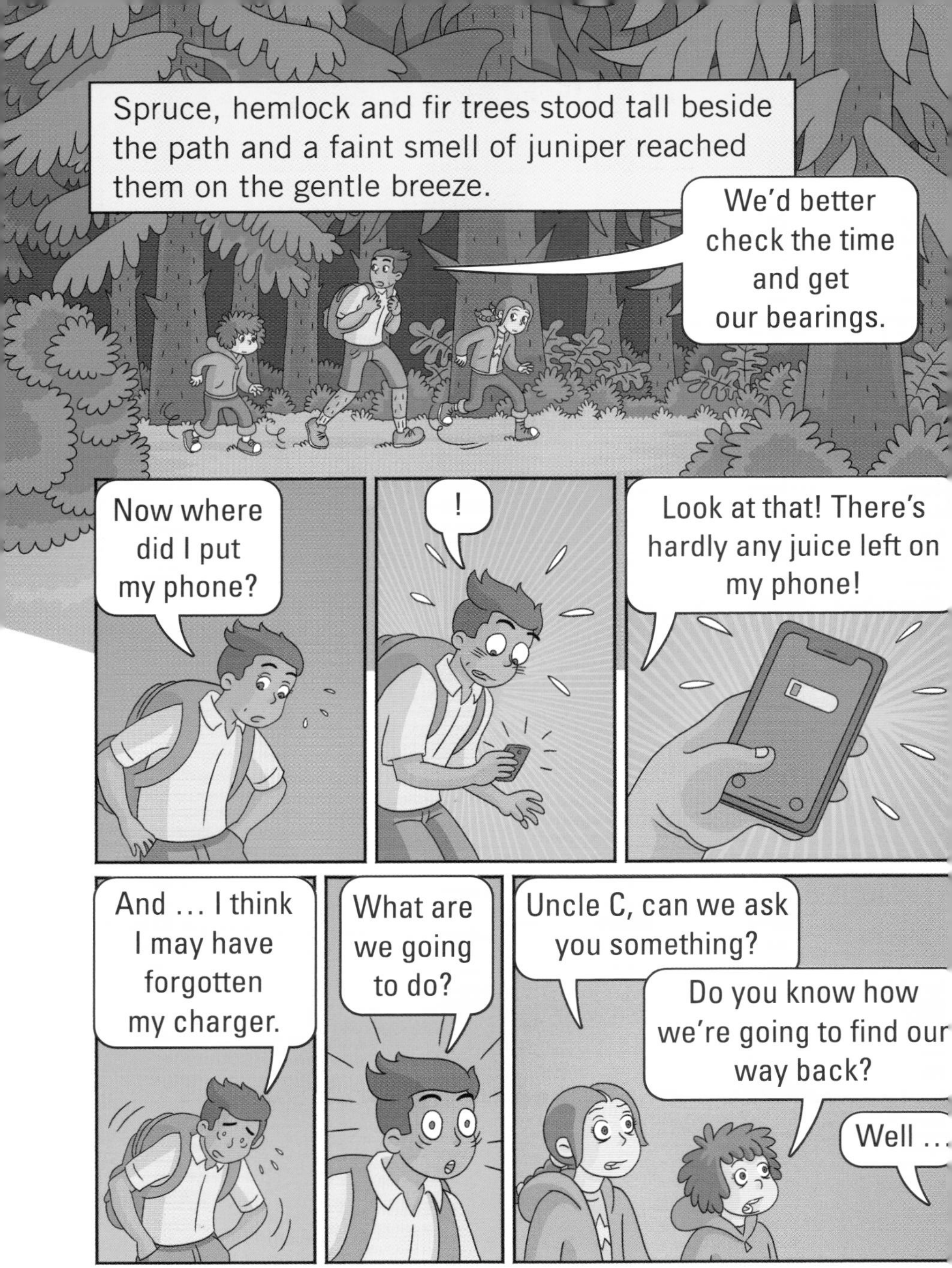
Spruce, hemlock and fir trees stood tall beside the path and a faint smell of juniper reached them on the gentle breeze.
We'd better check the time and get our bearings.
Now where did I put my phone?
!
Look at that! There's hardly any juice left on my phone!
And … I think I may have forgotten my charger.
What are we going to do?
Uncle C, can we ask you something?
Do you know how we're going to find our way back?
Well …

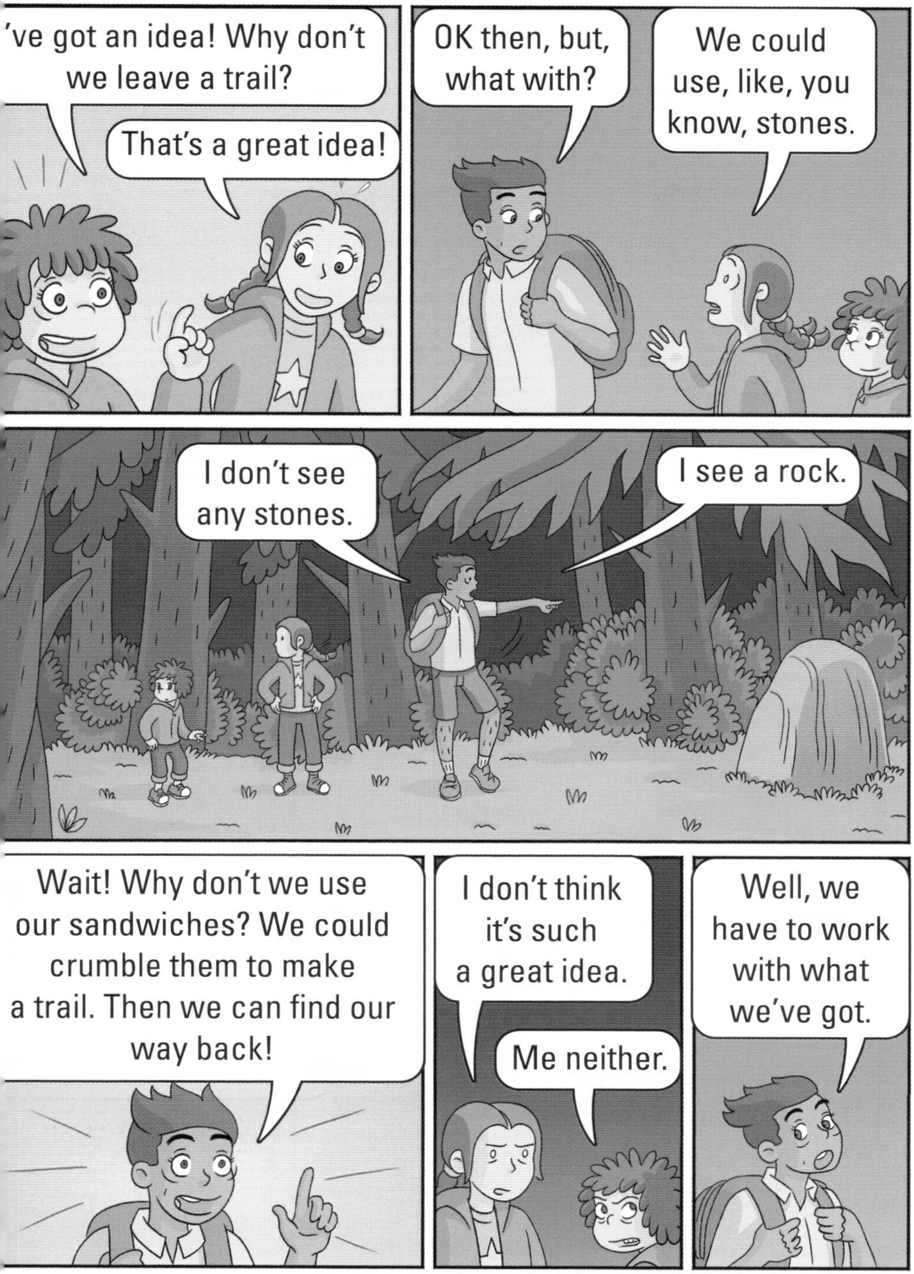
've got an idea! Why don't we leave a trail?
That's a great idea!
OK then, but, what with?
We could use, like, you know, stones.
I don't see any stones.
I see a rock.
Wait! Why don't we use our sandwiches? We could crumble them to make a trail. Then we can find our way back!
I don't think it's such a great idea.
Me neither.
Well, we have to work with what we've got.

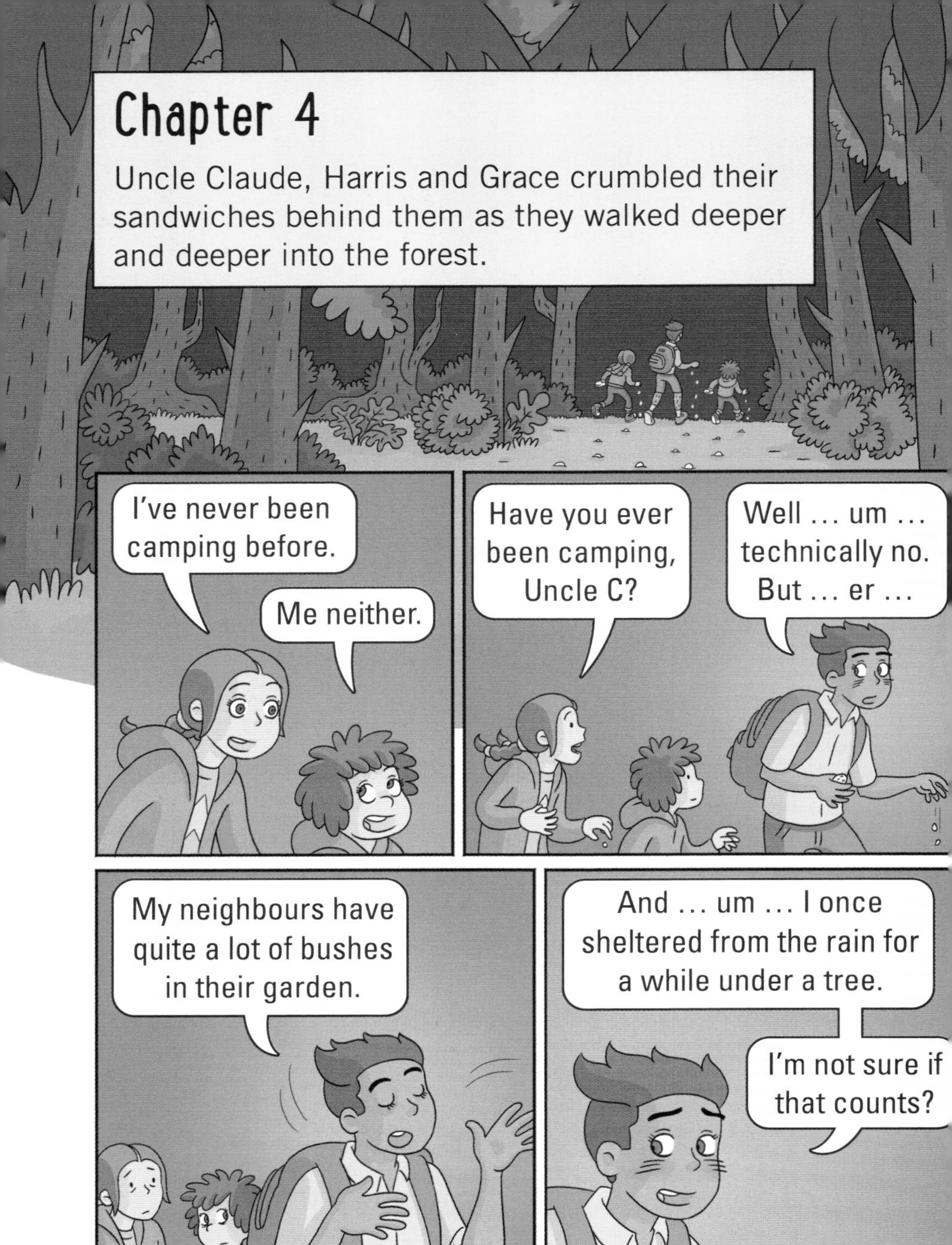
Chapter 4
Uncle Claude, Harris and Grace crumbled their sandwiches behind them as they walked deeper and deeper into the forest.
I've never been camping before.
Me neither.
Have you ever been camping, Uncle C?
Well … um … technically no. But … er …
My neighbours have quite a lot of bushes in their garden.
And … um … I once sheltered from the rain for a while under a tree.
I'm not sure if that counts?

They had been walking for at least an hour when Uncle Claude said ...

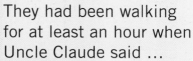

This bag may be small but it sure is heavy.

He had slowed down and become quite breathless.

OK! Time for a breather! I'm exhausted!

That was when Harris and Grace noticed something.

Oh oh!

Uncle C, I think we've got a problem.

What do you mean? What problem?

The trail of breadcrumbs.

It's all gone!

At least I can't see it.

I knew it was a bad idea!

Me too!

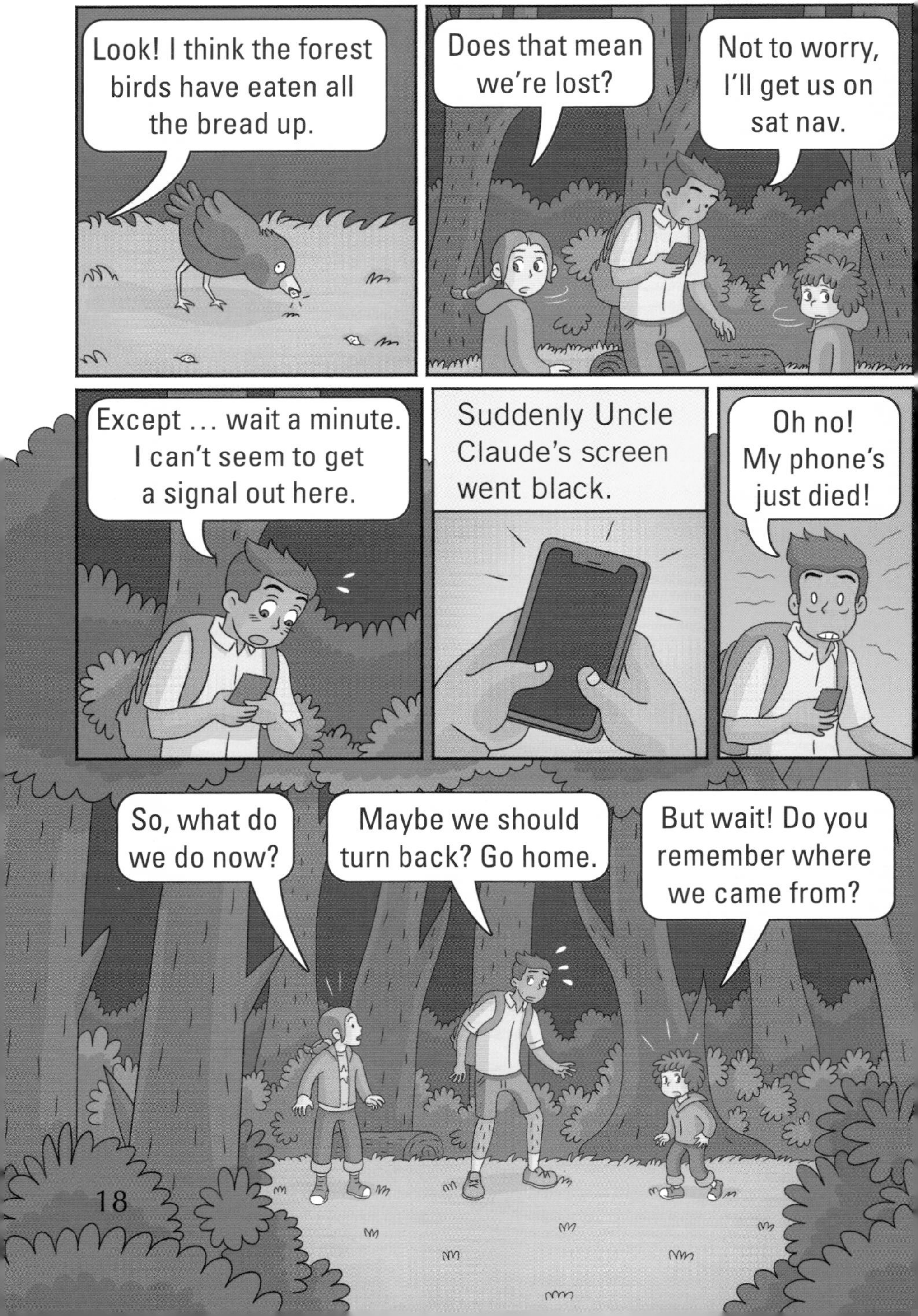

Look! I think the forest birds have eaten all the bread up.
Does that mean we're lost?
Not to worry, I'll get us on sat nav.
Except … wait a minute. I can't seem to get a signal out here.
Suddenly Uncle Claude's screen went black.
Oh no! My phone's just died!
So, what do we do now?
Maybe we should turn back? Go home.
But wait! Do you remember where we came from?

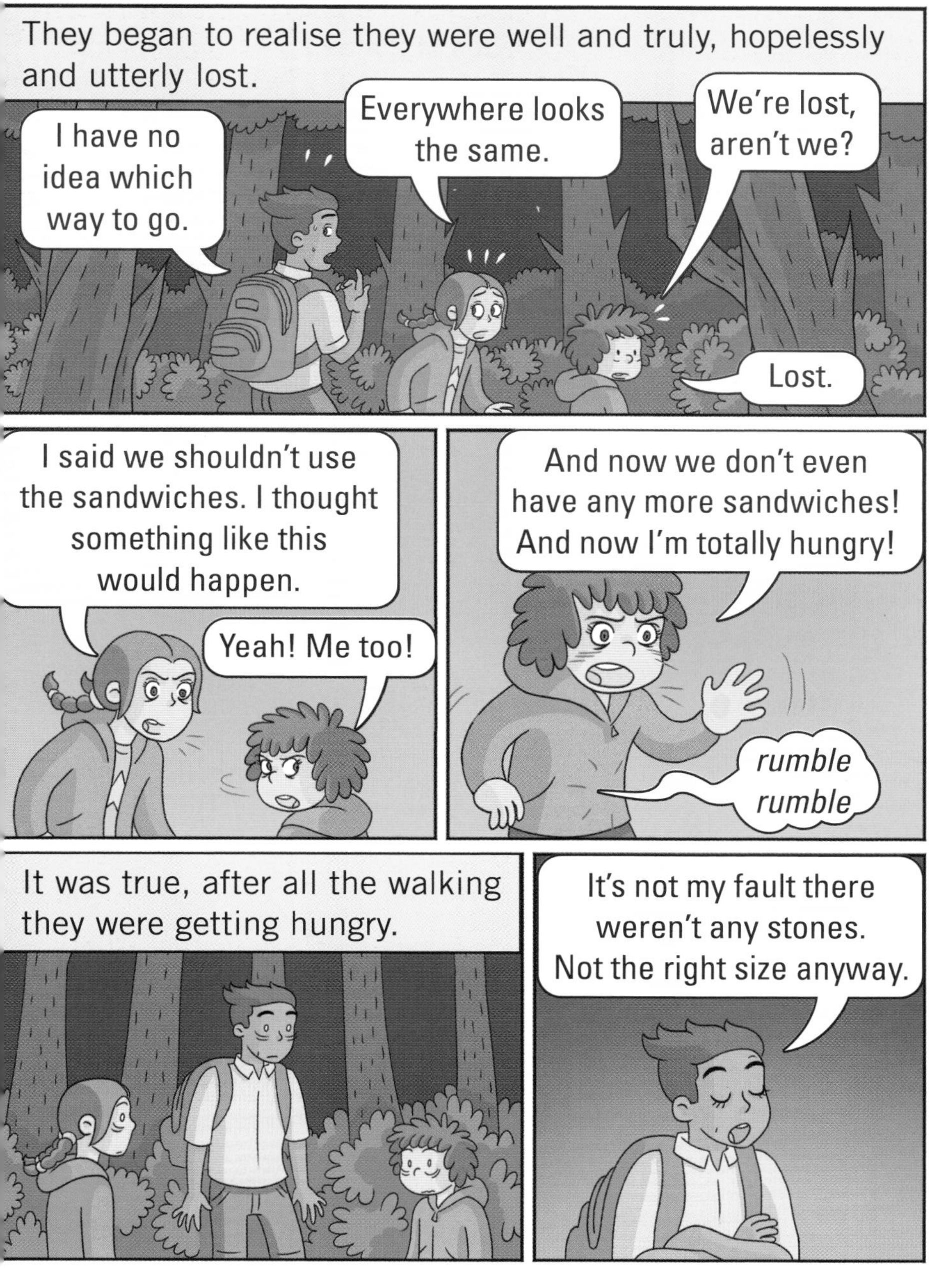
They began to realise they were well and truly, hopelessly and utterly lost.
I have no idea which way to go.
Everywhere looks the same.
We're lost, aren't we?
Lost.
I said we shouldn't use the sandwiches. I thought something like this would happen.
Yeah! Me too!
And now we don't even have any more sandwiches! And now I'm totally hungry!
rumble rumble
It was true, after all the walking they were getting hungry.
It's not my fault there weren't any stones. Not the right size anyway.

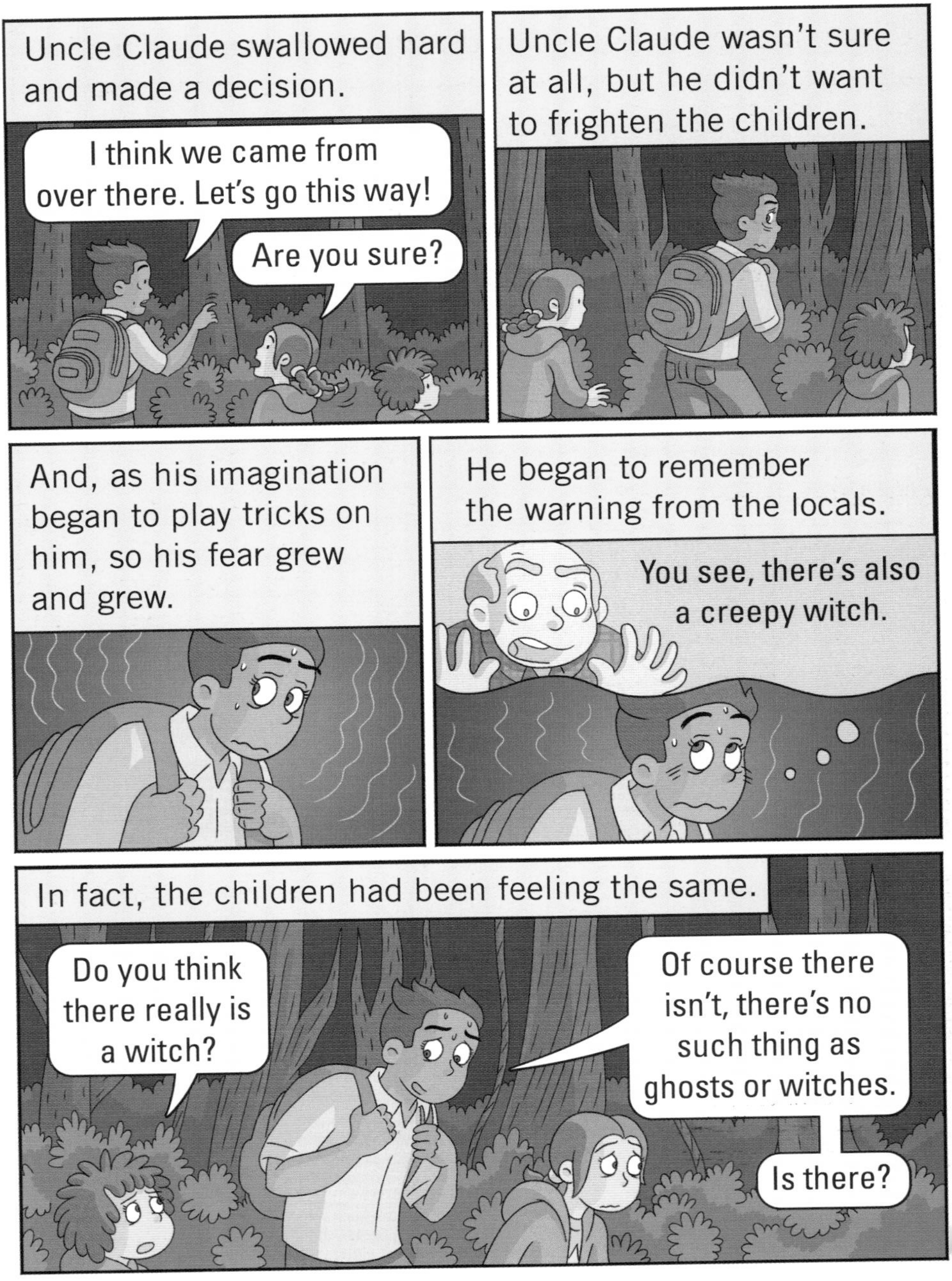

Uncle Claude swallowed hard and made a decision.
I think we came from over there. Let's go this way!
Are you sure?
Uncle Claude wasn't sure at all, but he didn't want to frighten the children.
And, as his imagination began to play tricks on him, so his fear grew and grew.
He began to remember the warning from the locals.
You see, there's also a creepy witch.
In fact, the children had been feeling the same.
Do you think there really is a witch?
Of course there isn't, there's no such thing as ghosts or witches.
Is there?

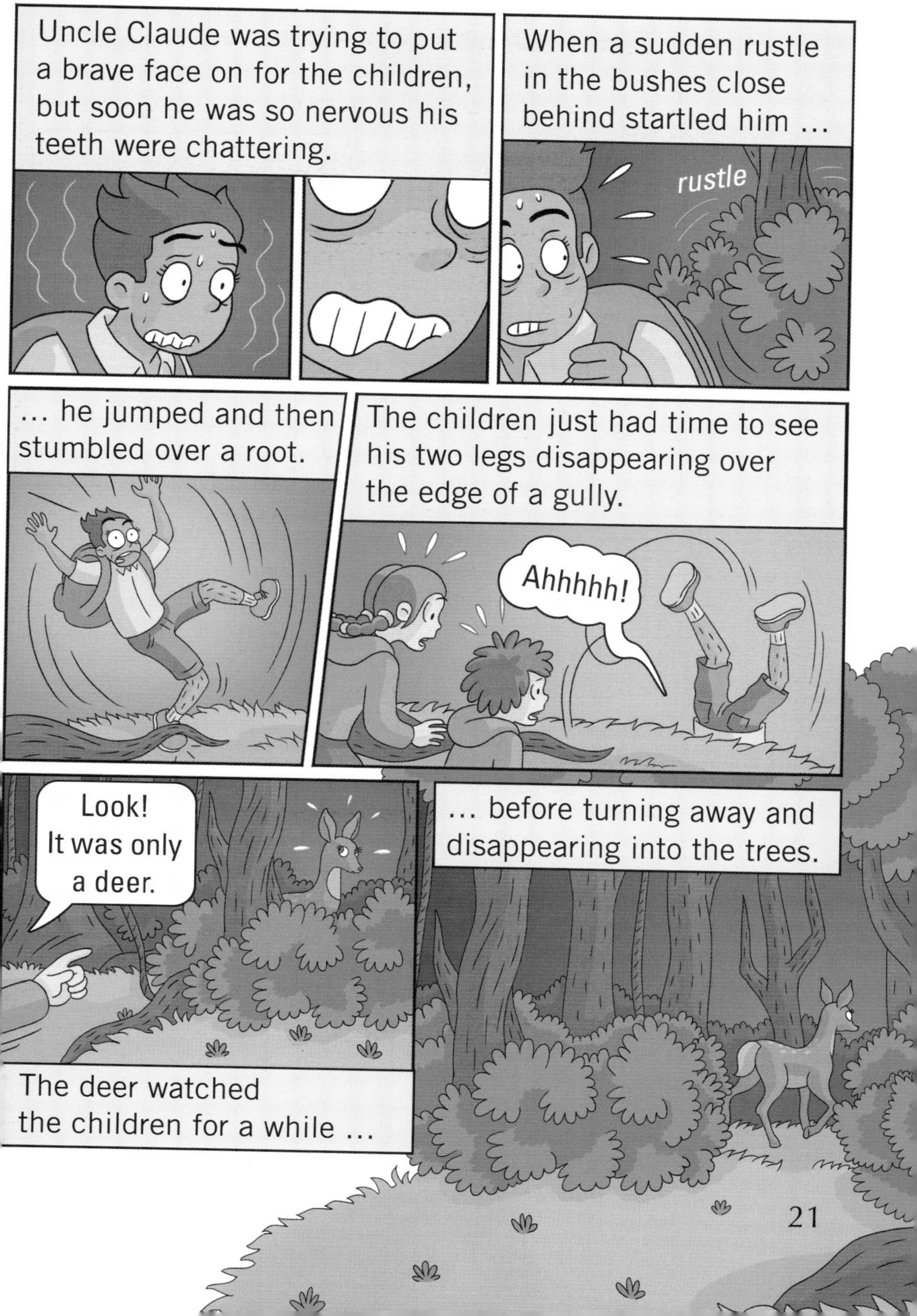
Uncle Claude was trying to put a brave face on for the children, but soon he was so nervous his teeth were chattering.
When a sudden rustle in the bushes close behind startled him …
rustle
… he jumped and then stumbled over a root.
The children just had time to see his two legs disappearing over the edge of a gully.
Ahhhhh!
Look! It was only a deer.
The deer watched the children for a while …
… before turning away and disappearing into the trees.

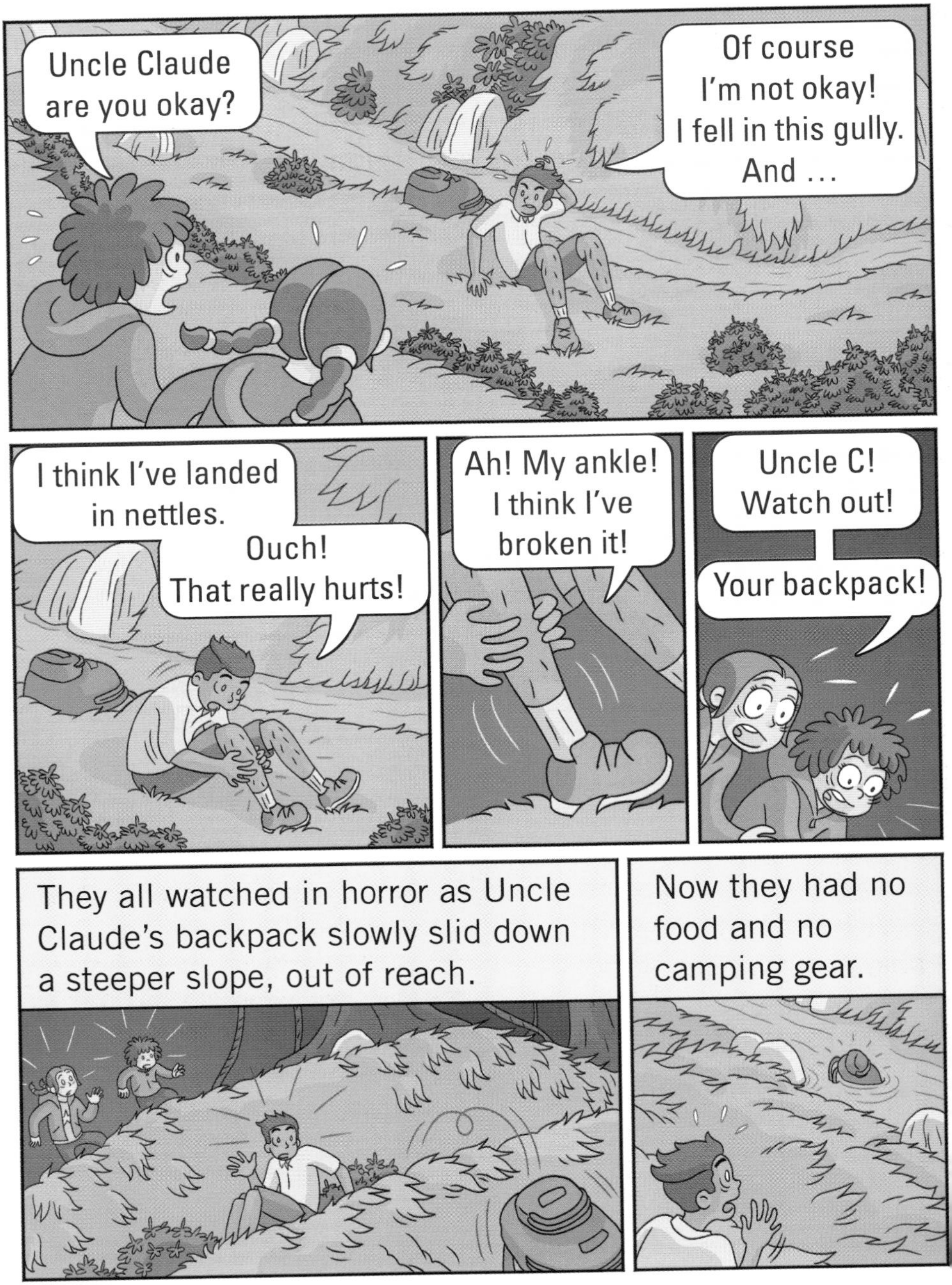
Uncle Claude are you okay?
Of course I'm not okay! I fell in this gully. And …
I think I've landed in nettles.
Ouch! That really hurts!
Ah! My ankle! I think I've broken it!
Uncle C! Watch out!
Your backpack!
They all watched in horror as Uncle Claude's backpack slowly slid down a steeper slope, out of reach.
Now they had no food and no camping gear.

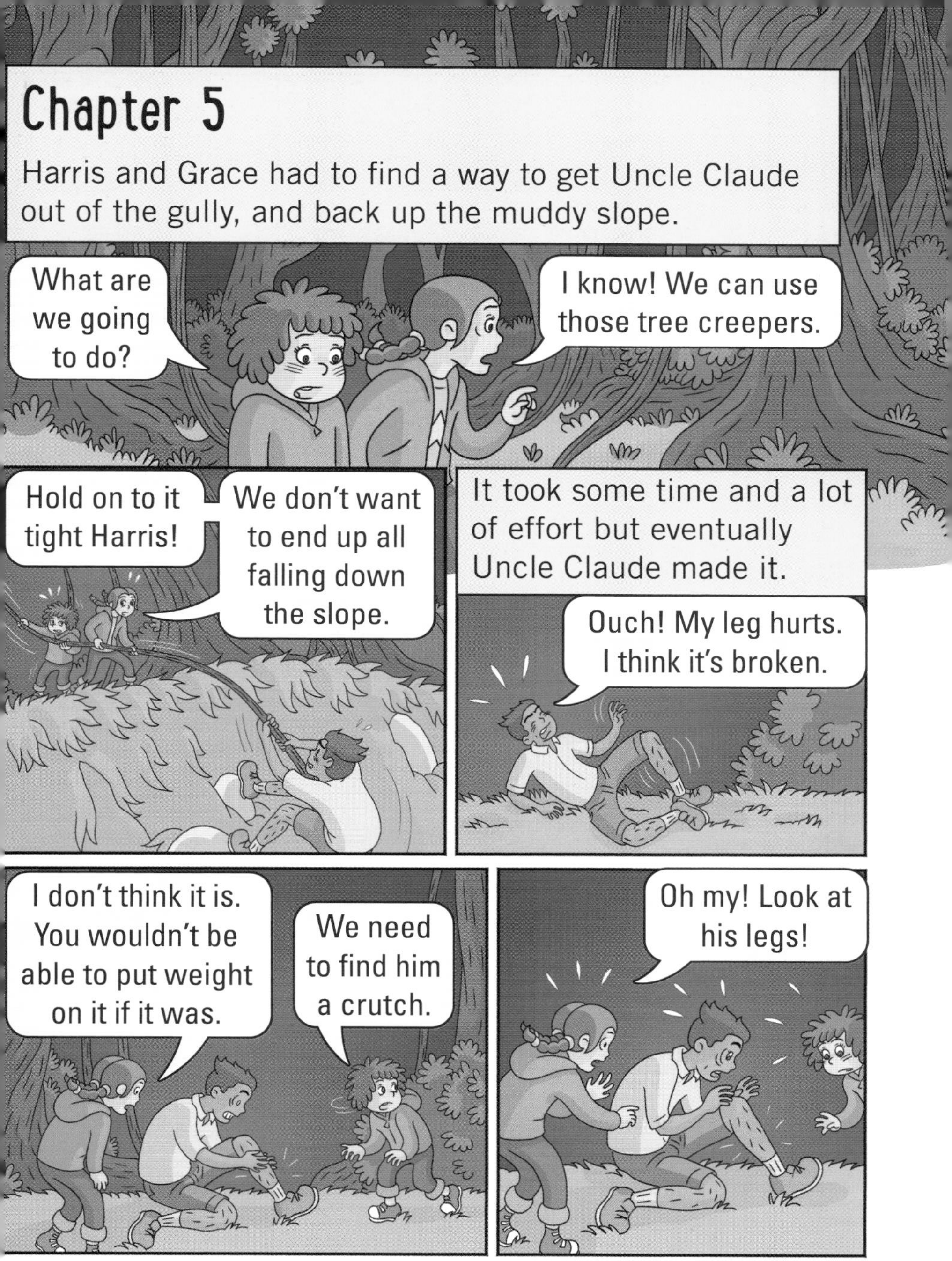
Chapter 5
Harris and Grace had to find a way to get Uncle Claude out of the gully, and back up the muddy slope.
What are we going to do?
I know! We can use those tree creepers.
Hold on to it tight Harris!
We don't want to end up all falling down the slope.
It took some time and a lot of effort but eventually Uncle Claude made it.
Ouch! My leg hurts. I think it's broken.
I don't think it is. You wouldn't be able to put weight on it if it was.
We need to find him a crutch.
Oh my! Look at his legs!

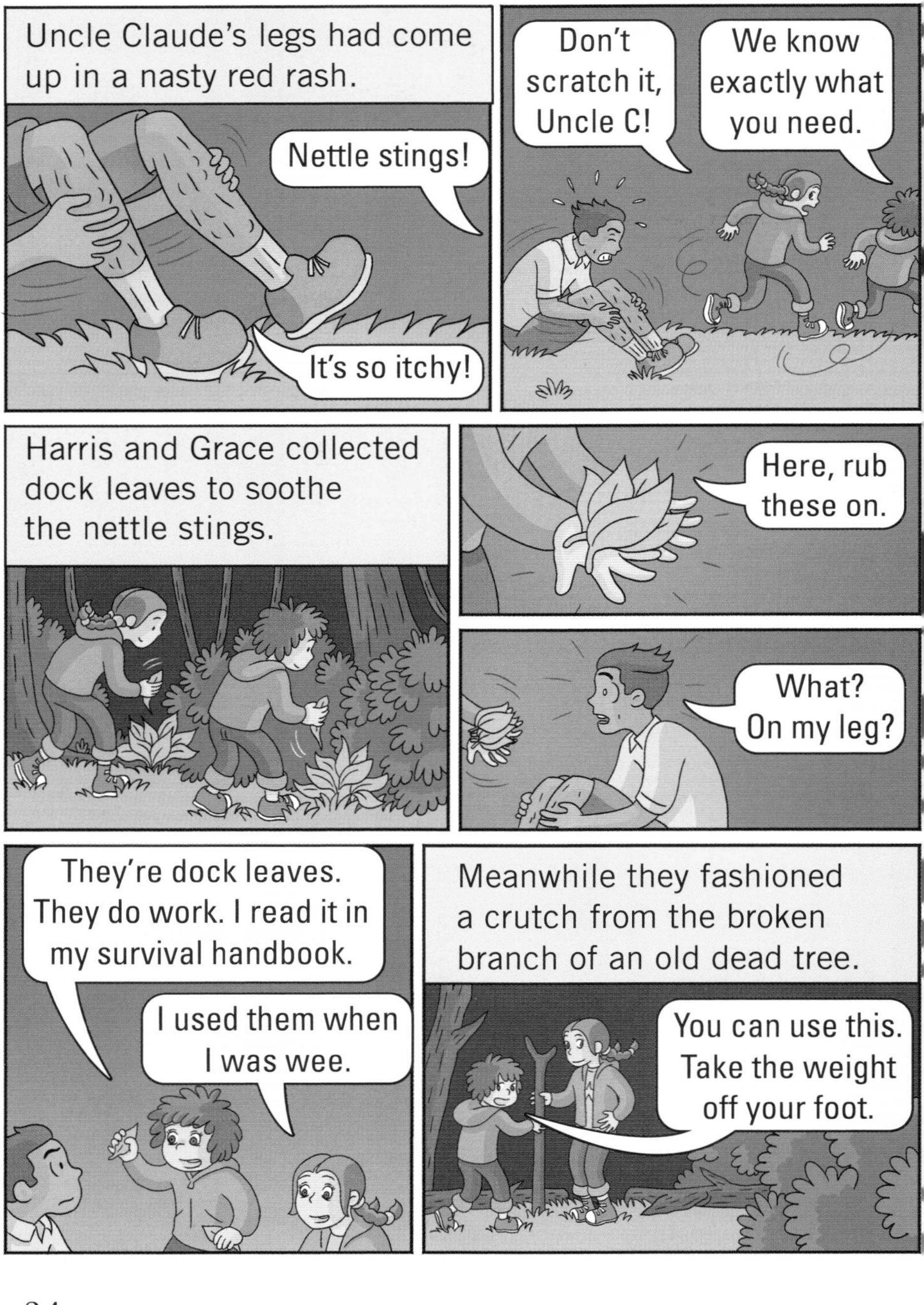
Uncle Claude's legs had come up in a nasty red rash.
Nettle stings!
It's so itchy!
Don't scratch it, Uncle C!
We know exactly what you need.
Harris and Grace collected dock leaves to soothe the nettle stings.
Here, rub these on.
What? On my leg?
They're dock leaves. They do work. I read it in my survival handbook.
I used them when I was wee.
Meanwhile they fashioned a crutch from the broken branch of an old dead tree.
You can use this. Take the weight off your foot.

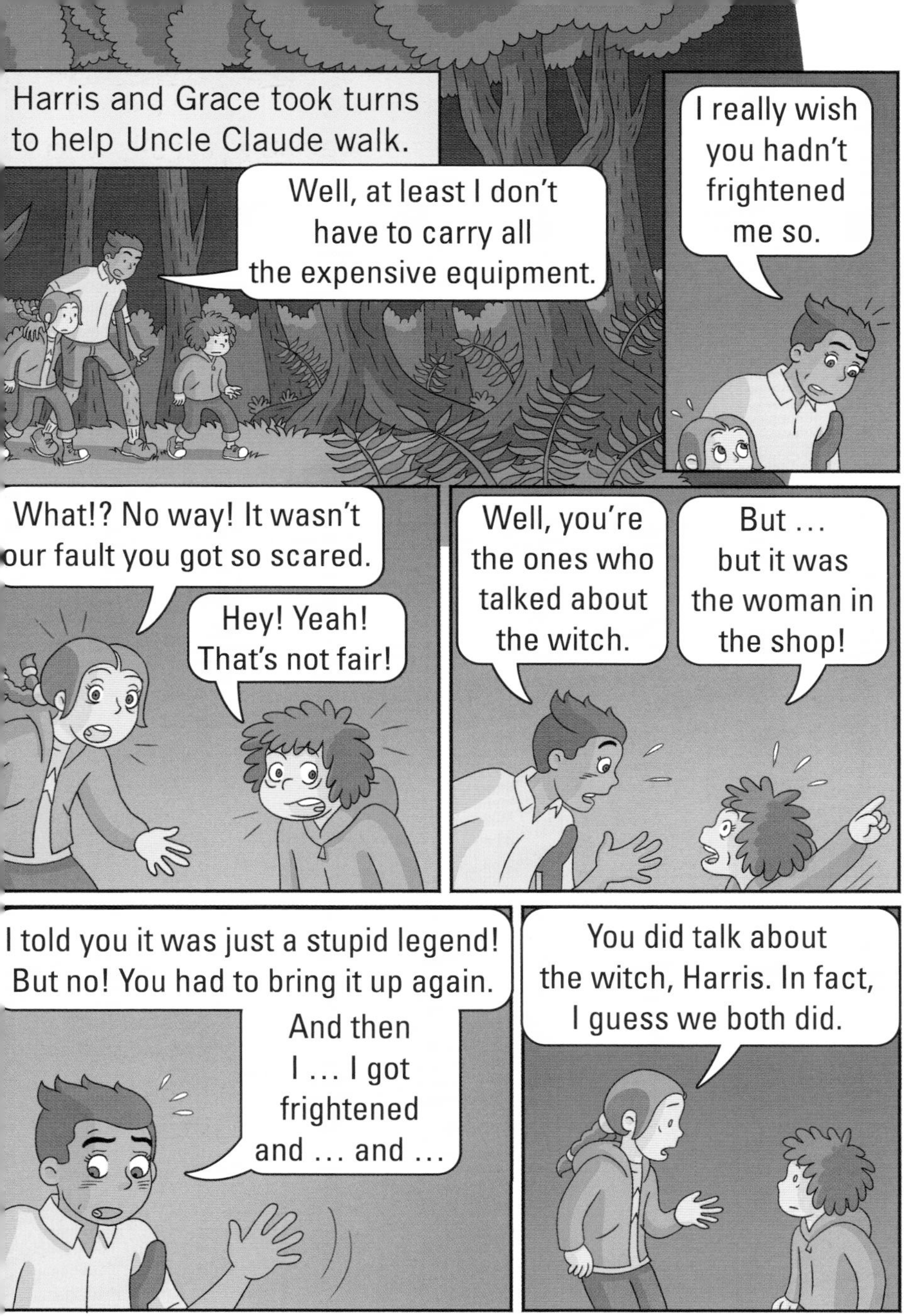
Harris and Grace took turns to help Uncle Claude walk.
Well, at least I don't have to carry all the expensive equipment.
I really wish you hadn't frightened me so.
What!? No way! It wasn't our fault you got so scared.
Hey! Yeah! That's not fair!
Well, you're the ones who talked about the witch.
But … but it was the woman in the shop!
I told you it was just a stupid legend! But no! You had to bring it up again.
And then I … I got frightened and … and …
You did talk about the witch, Harris. In fact, I guess we both did.

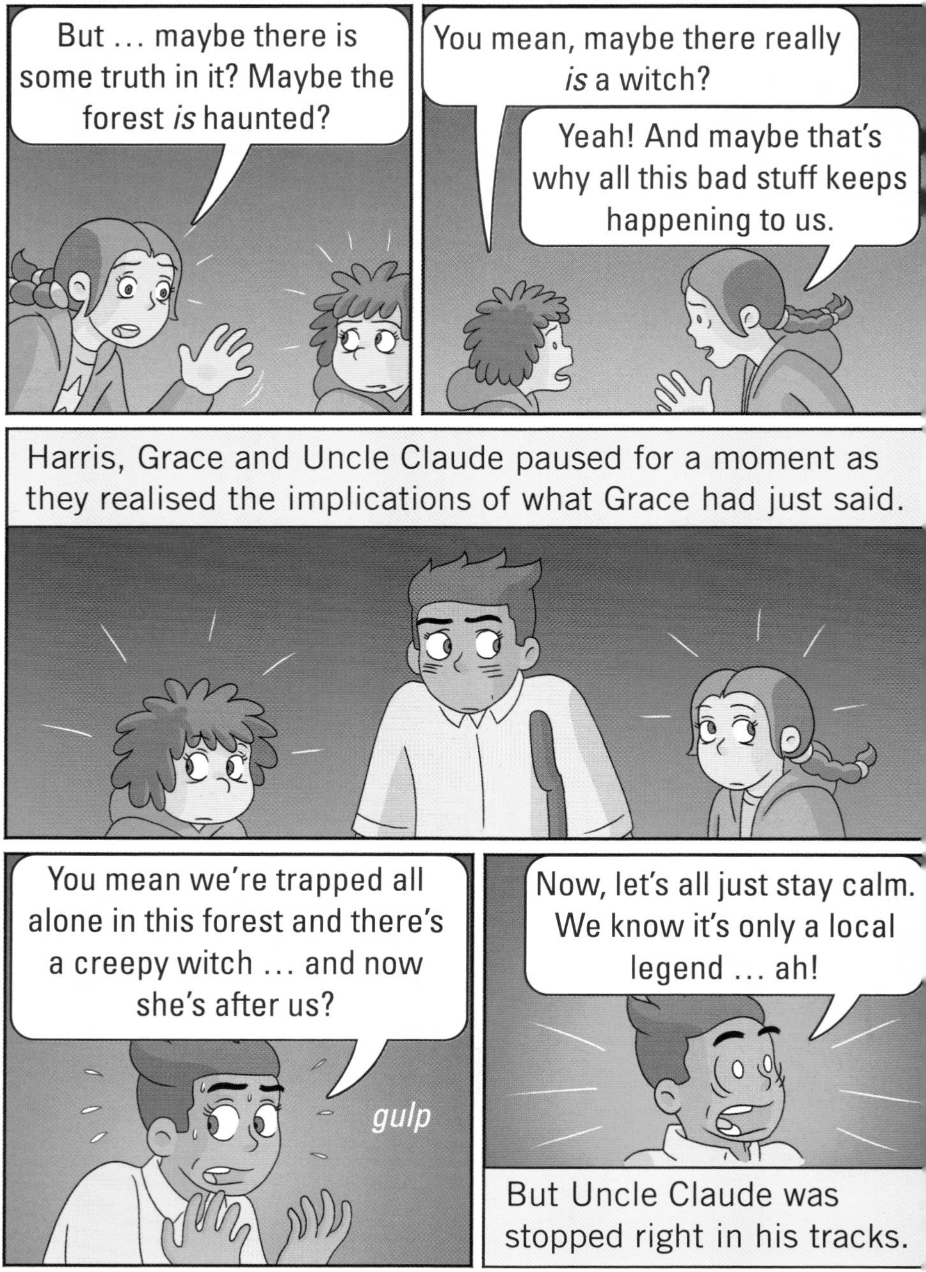
But … maybe there is some truth in it? Maybe the forest *is* haunted?
You mean, maybe there really *is* a witch?
Yeah! And maybe that's why all this bad stuff keeps happening to us.
Harris, Grace and Uncle Claude paused for a moment as they realised the implications of what Grace had just said.
You mean we're trapped all alone in this forest and there's a creepy witch … and now she's after us?
gulp
Now, let's all just stay calm. We know it's only a local legend … ah!
But Uncle Claude was stopped right in his tracks.

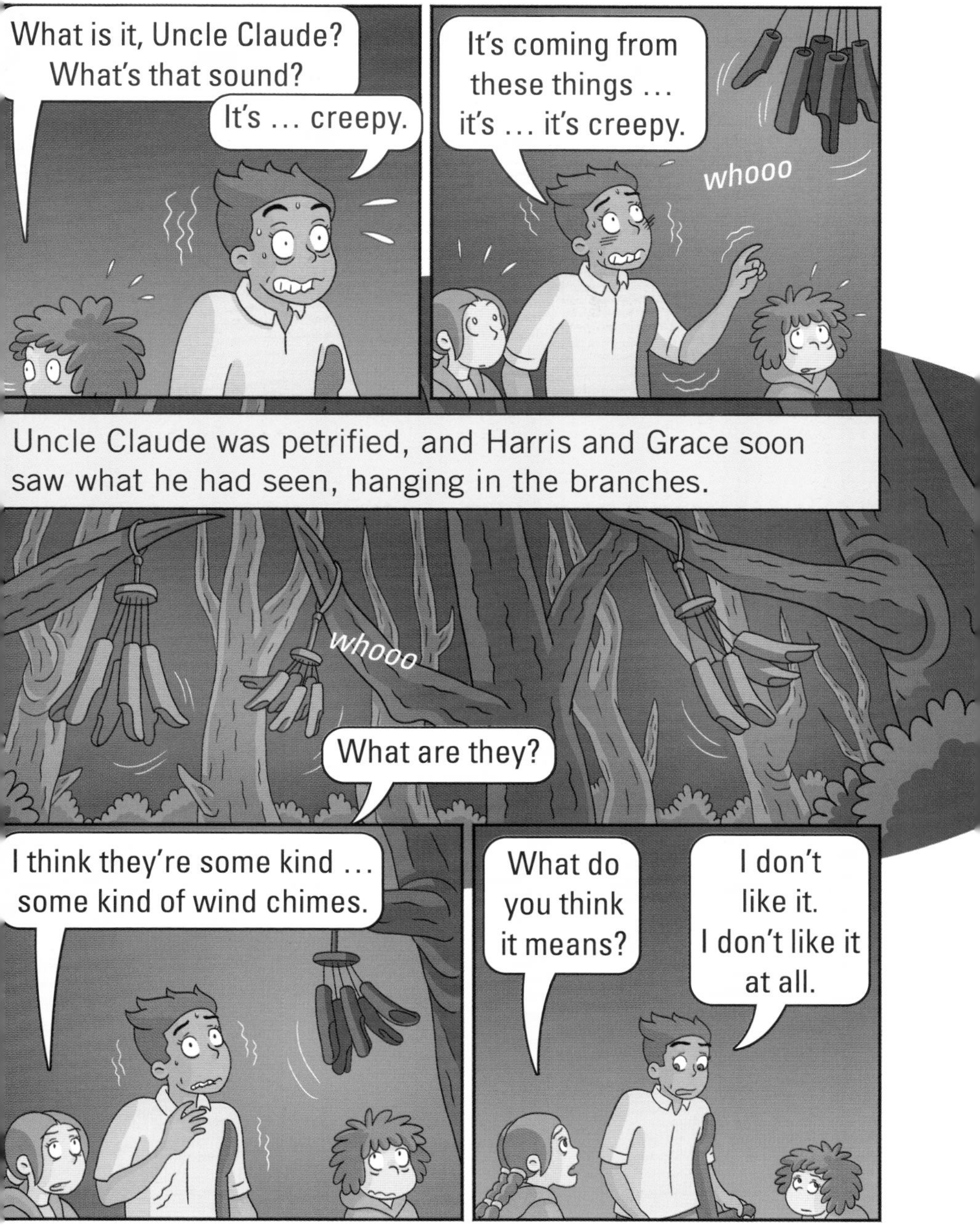
What is it, Uncle Claude? What's that sound?
It's … creepy.
It's coming from these things … it's … it's creepy.
whooo
Uncle Claude was petrified, and Harris and Grace soon saw what he had seen, hanging in the branches.
whooo
What are they?
I think they're some kind … some kind of wind chimes.
What do you think it means?
I don't like it. I don't like it at all.

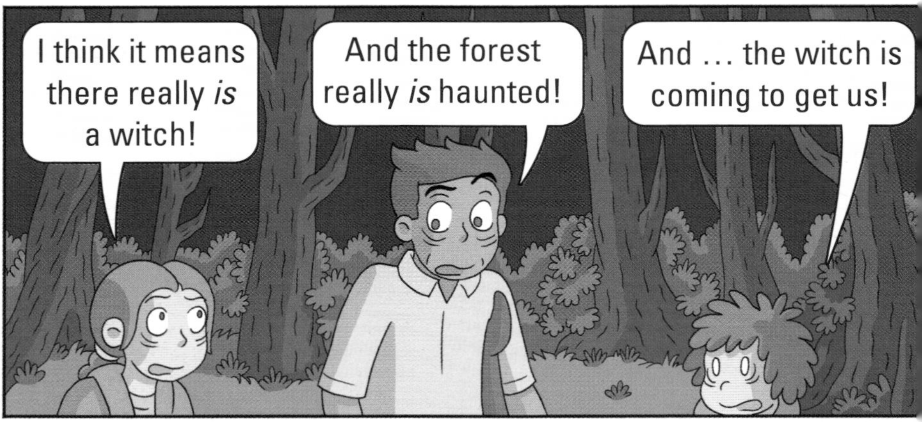
I think it means there really *is* a witch!
And the forest really *is* haunted!
And … the witch is coming to get us!

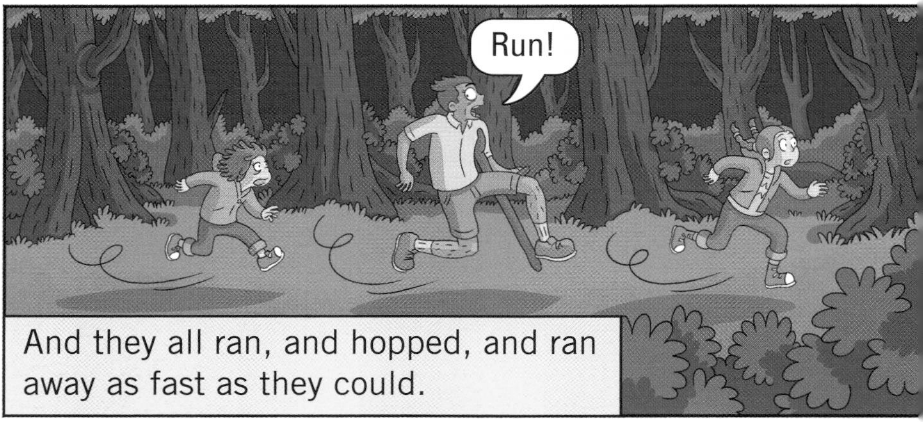
Run!
And they all ran, and hopped, and ran away as fast as they could.

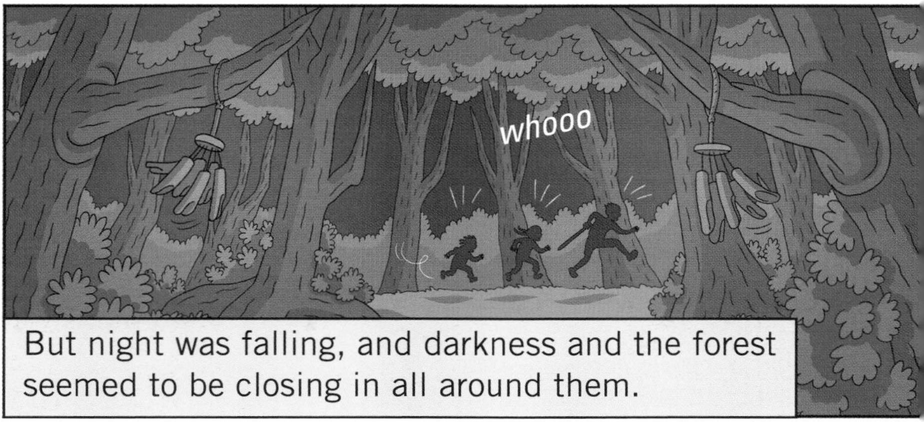
whooo
But night was falling, and darkness and the forest seemed to be closing in all around them.

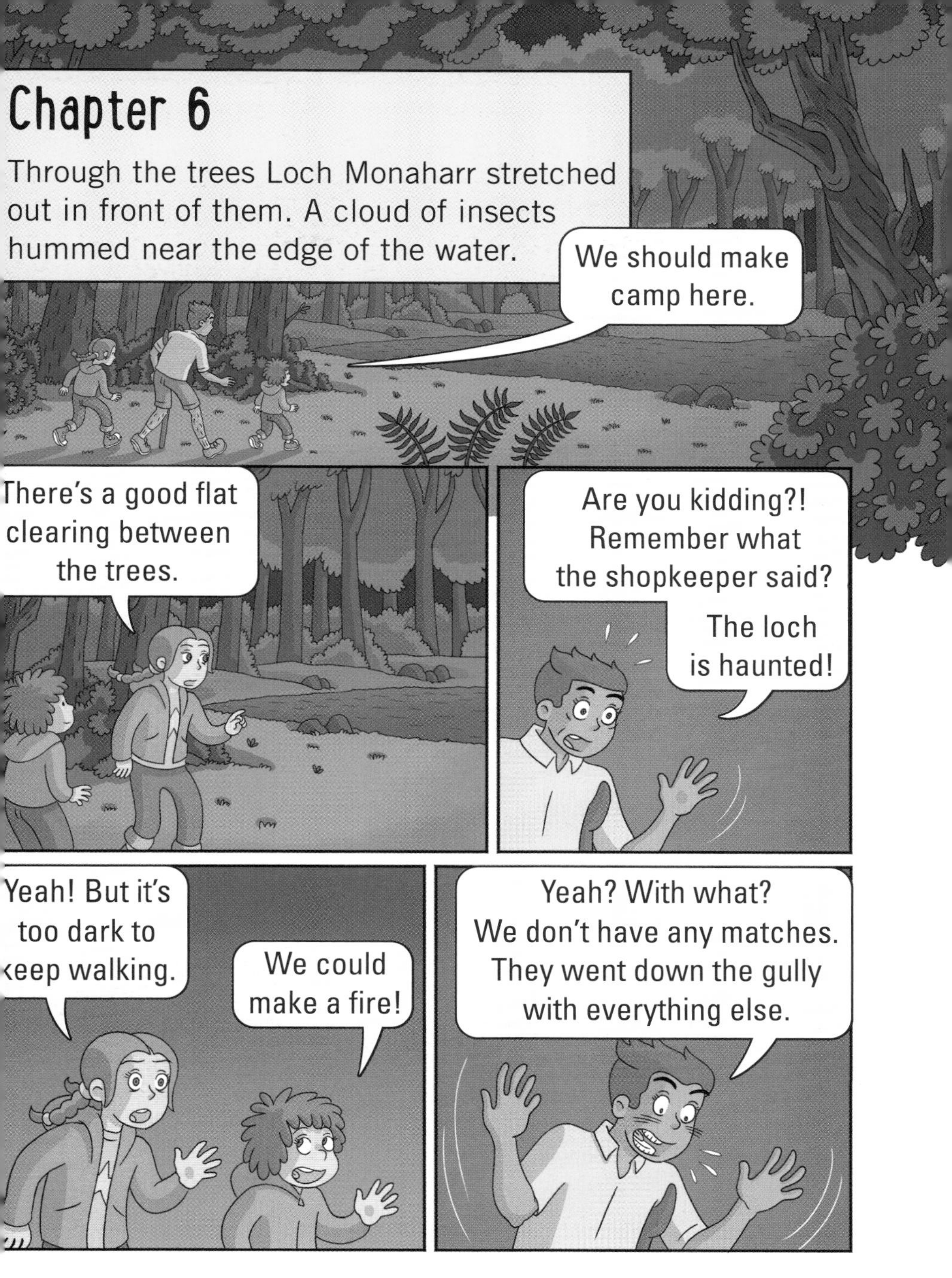
Chapter 6
Through the trees Loch Monaharr stretched out in front of them. A cloud of insects hummed near the edge of the water.
We should make camp here.
There's a good flat clearing between the trees.
Are you kidding?! Remember what the shopkeeper said?
The loch is haunted!
Yeah! But it's too dark to keep walking.
We could make a fire!
Yeah? With what? We don't have any matches. They went down the gully with everything else.

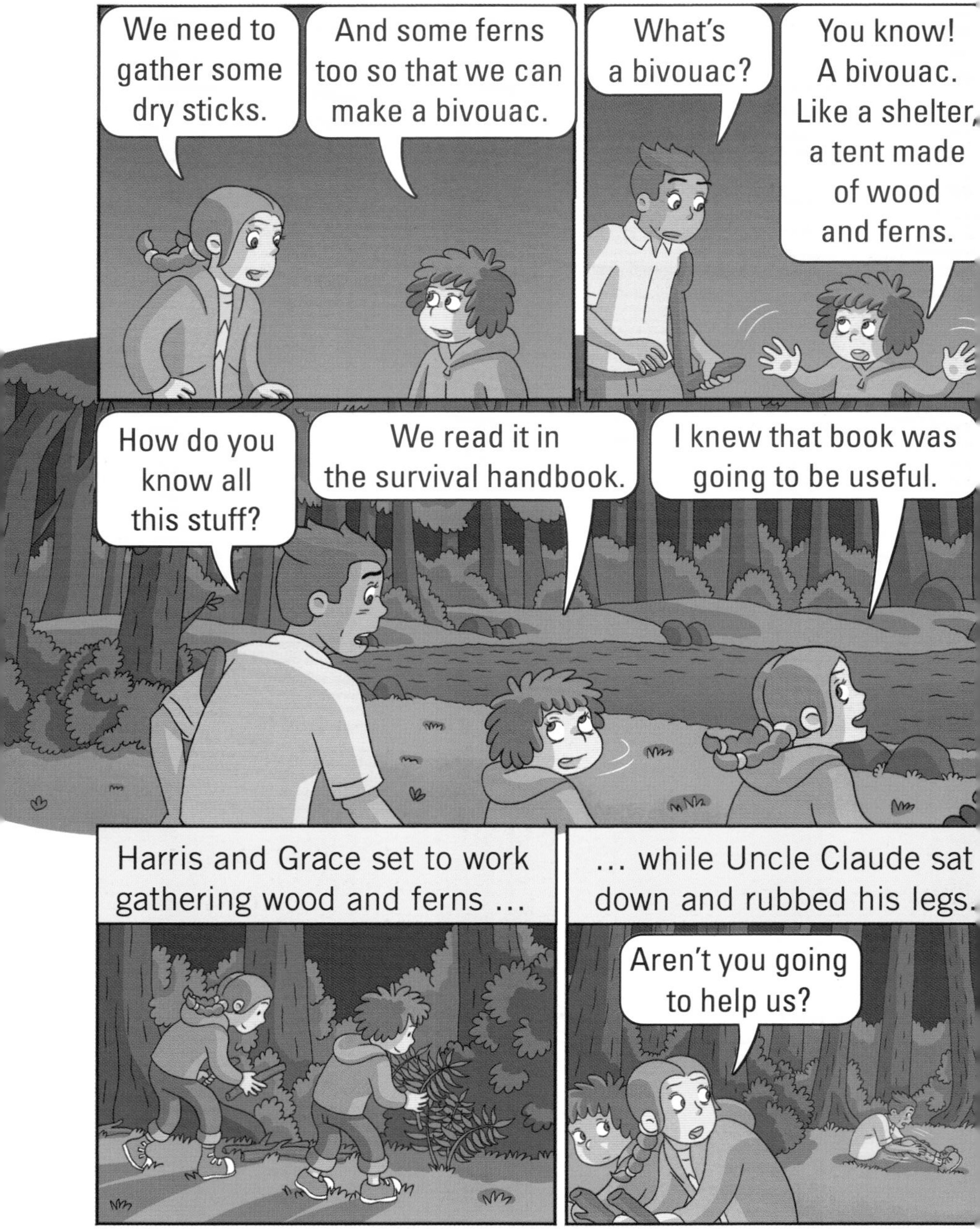
We need to gather some dry sticks.
And some ferns too so that we can make a bivouac.
What's a bivouac?
You know! A bivouac. Like a shelter, a tent made of wood and ferns.
How do you know all this stuff?
We read it in the survival handbook.
I knew that book was going to be useful.
Harris and Grace set to work gathering wood and ferns …
… while Uncle Claude sat down and rubbed his legs.
Aren't you going to help us?

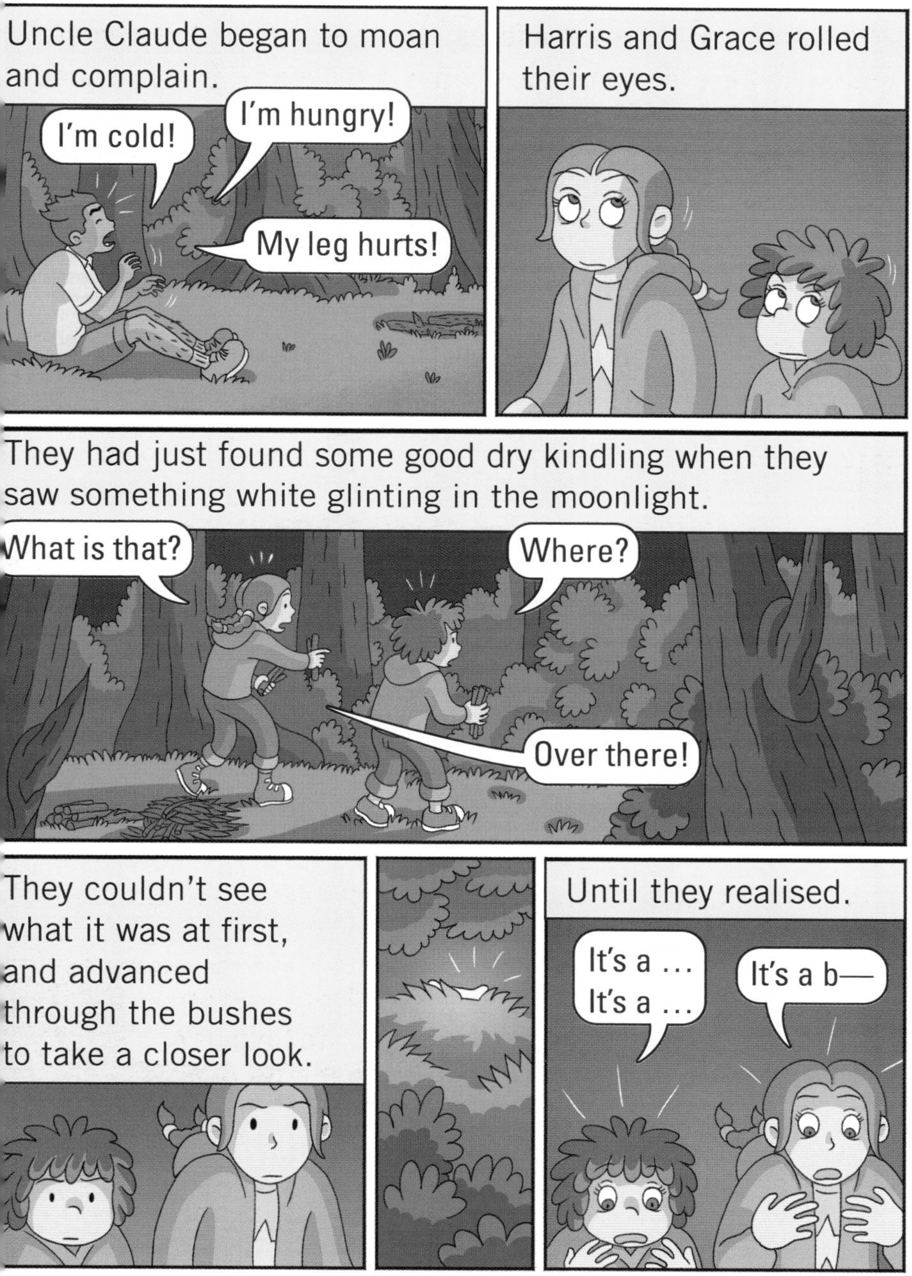
Uncle Claude began to moan and complain.
I'm cold!
I'm hungry!
My leg hurts!
Harris and Grace rolled their eyes.
They had just found some good dry kindling when they saw something white glinting in the moonlight.
What is that?
Where?
Over there!
They couldn't see what it was at first, and advanced through the bushes to take a closer look.
Until they realised.
It's a …
It's a …
It's a b—

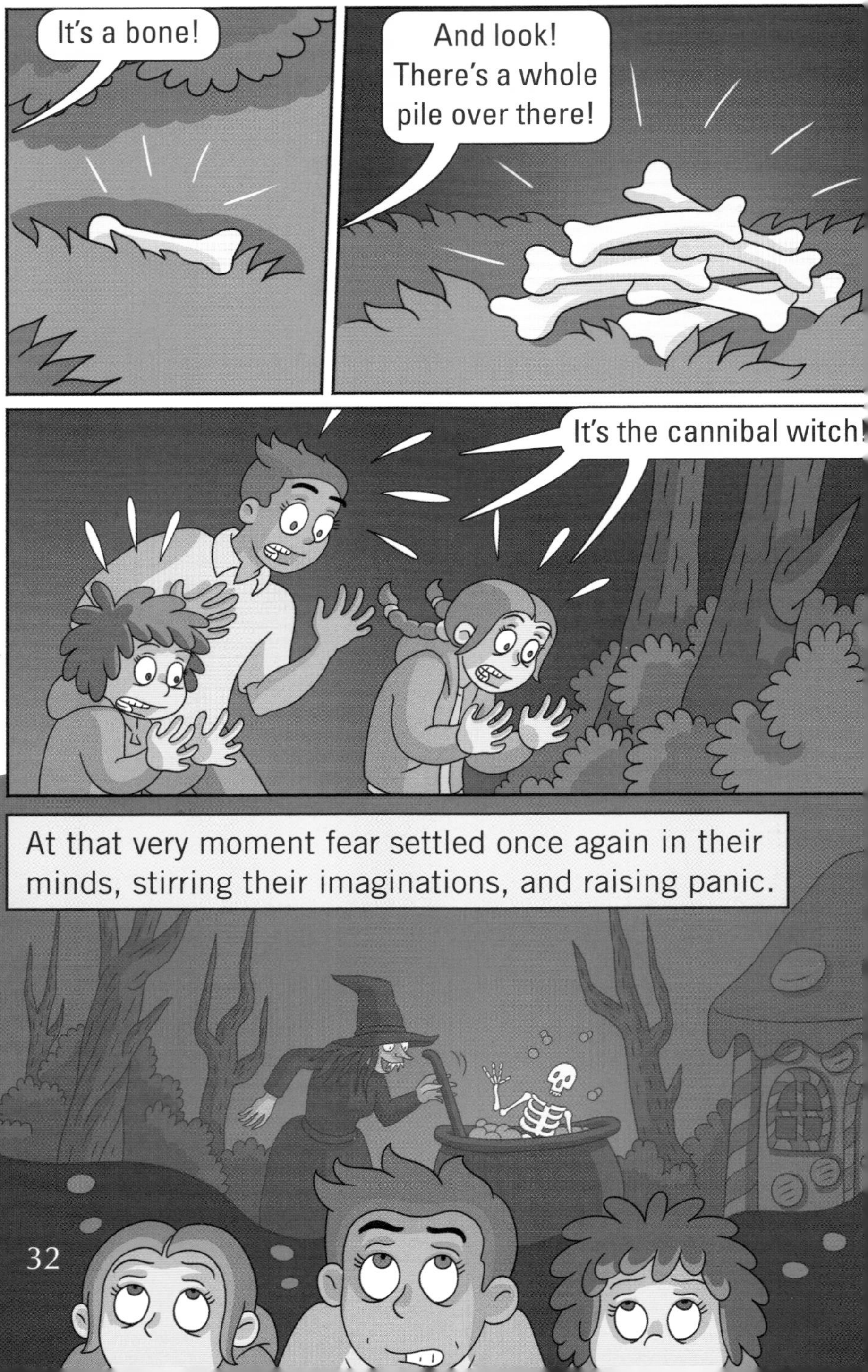
It's a bone!
And look! There's a whole pile over there!
It's the cannibal witch!
At that very moment fear settled once again in their minds, stirring their imaginations, and raising panic.

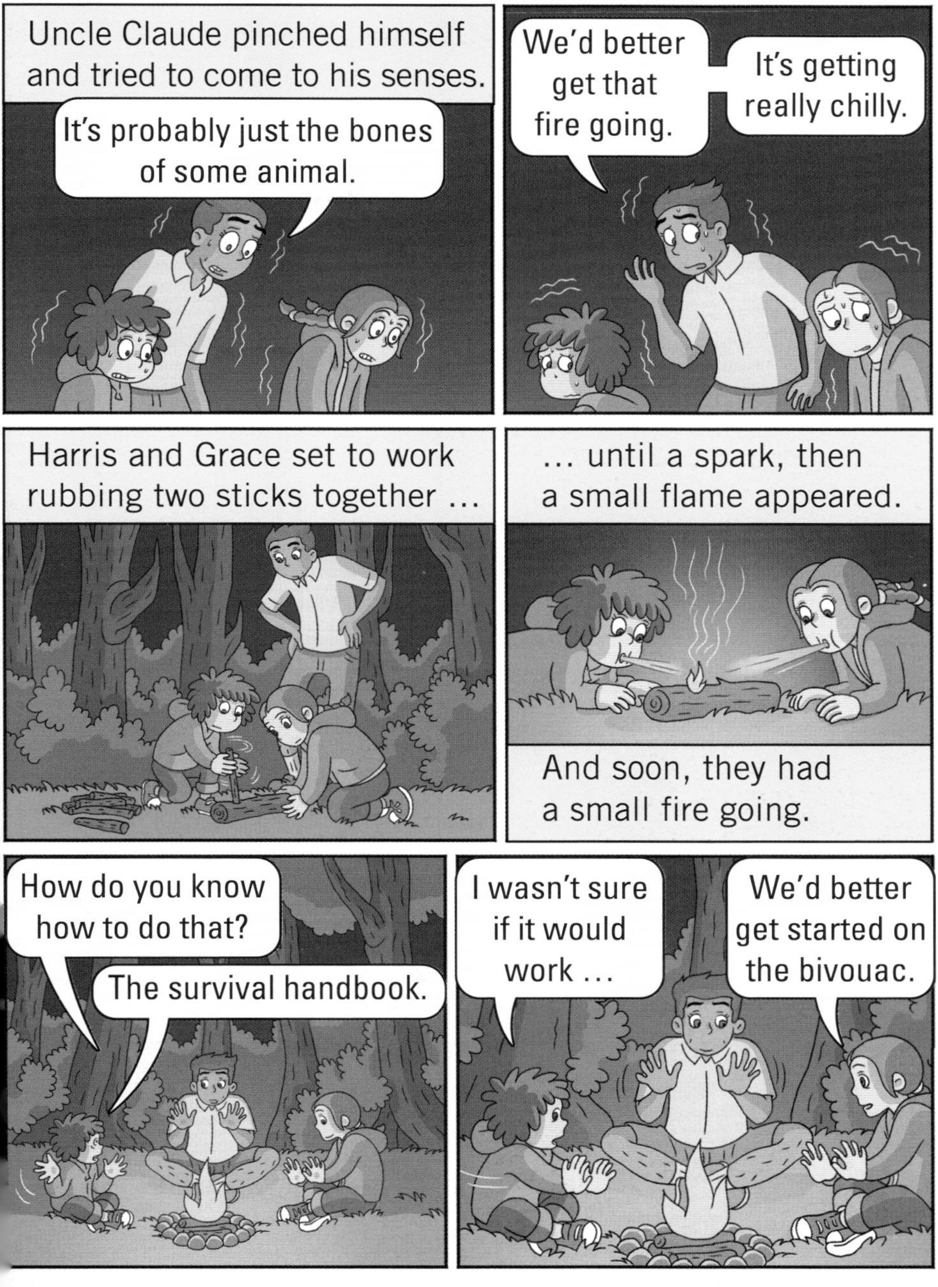
Uncle Claude pinched himself and tried to come to his senses.
It's probably just the bones of some animal.
We'd better get that fire going.
It's getting really chilly.
Harris and Grace set to work rubbing two sticks together …
… until a spark, then a small flame appeared.
And soon, they had a small fire going.
How do you know how to do that?
The survival handbook.
I wasn't sure if it would work …
We'd better get started on the bivouac.

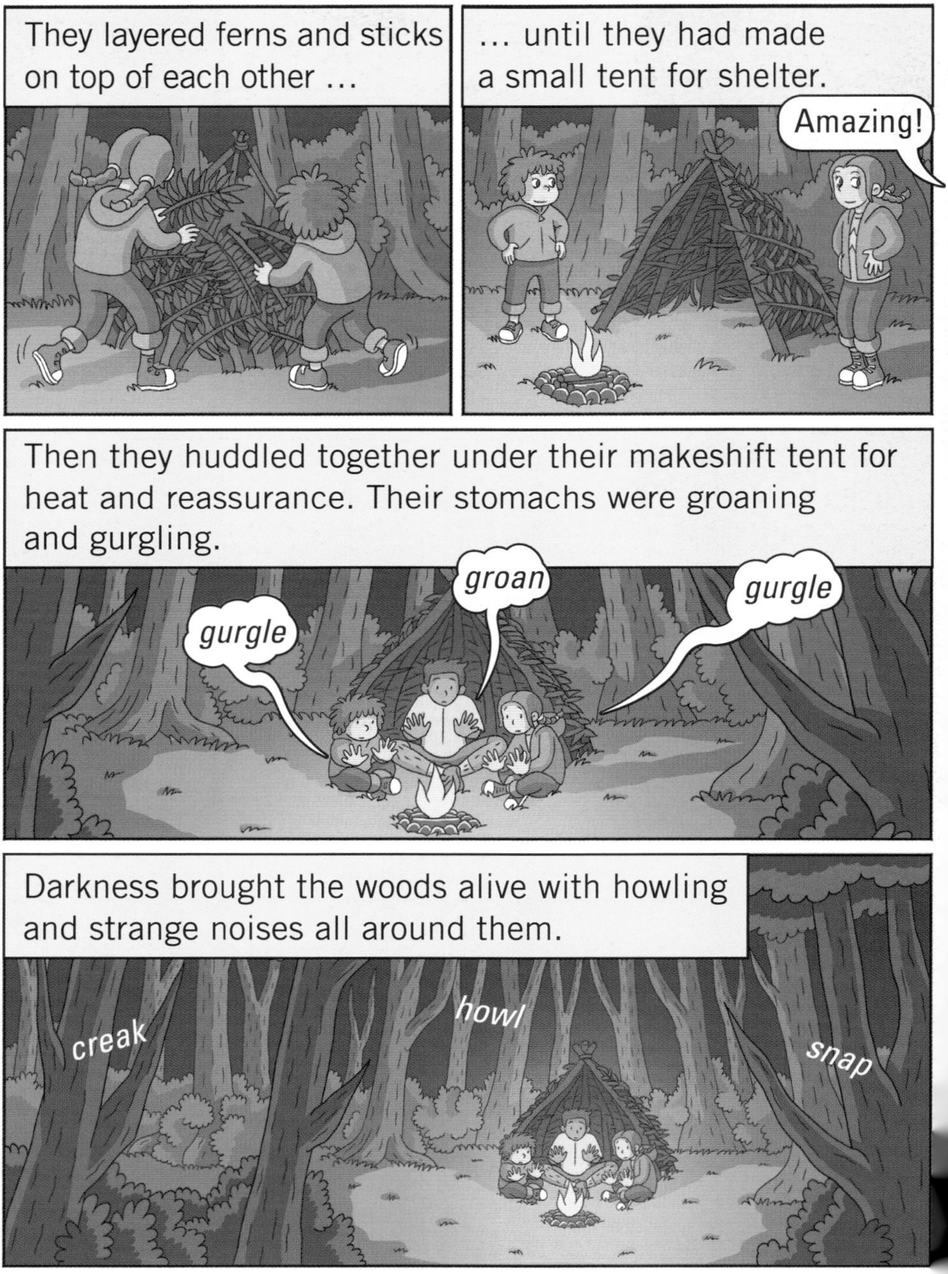
They layered ferns and sticks on top of each other …
… until they had made a small tent for shelter.
Amazing!
Then they huddled together under their makeshift tent for heat and reassurance. Their stomachs were groaning and gurgling.
gurgle
groan
gurgle
Darkness brought the woods alive with howling and strange noises all around them.
creak
howl
snap

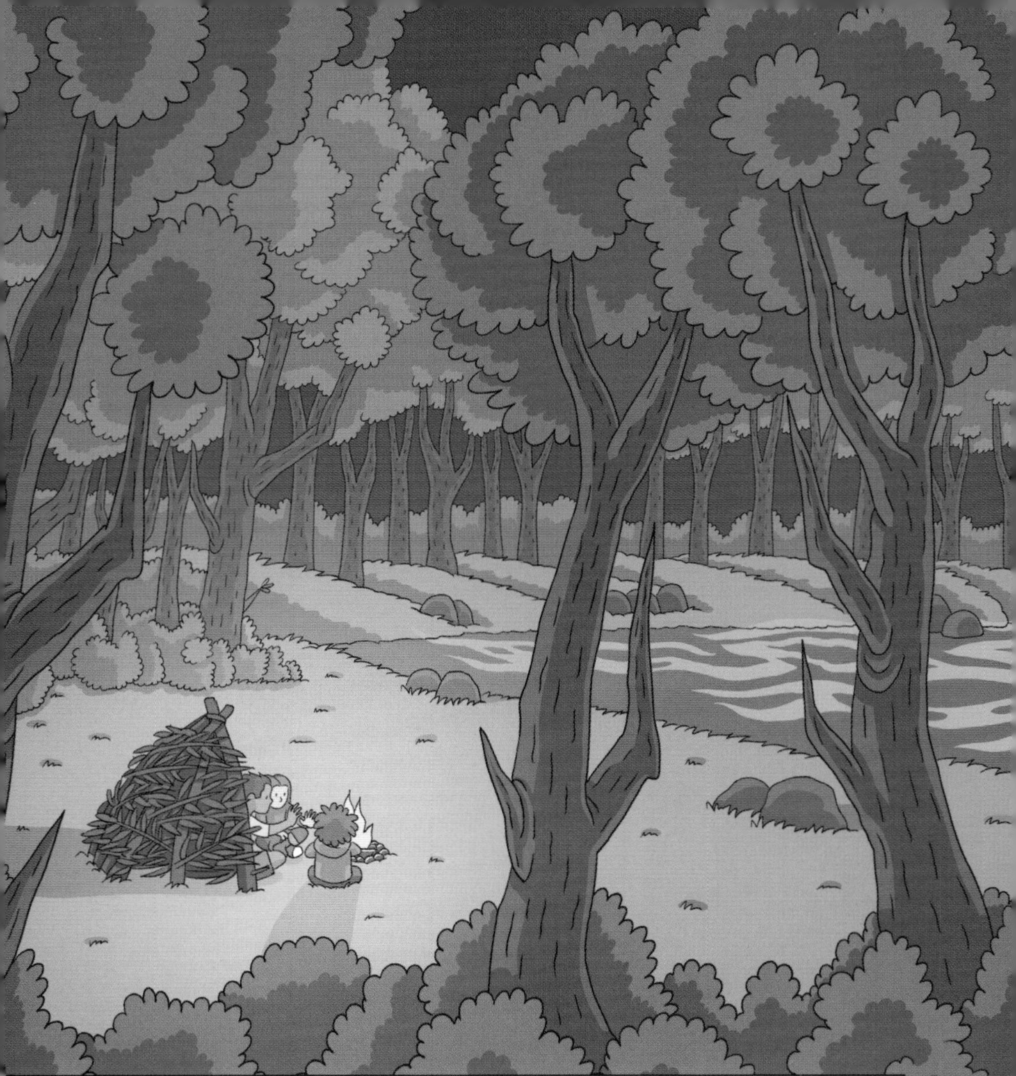

Shrouds of mist slowly gathered on the surface of Loch Monaharr, swirling and shifting on the water. As they all thought about the shopkeeper's warning, Harris and Grace remembered that they'd once heard a legend that said that fog on a loch was in fact ghosts. They didn't tell Uncle Claude.

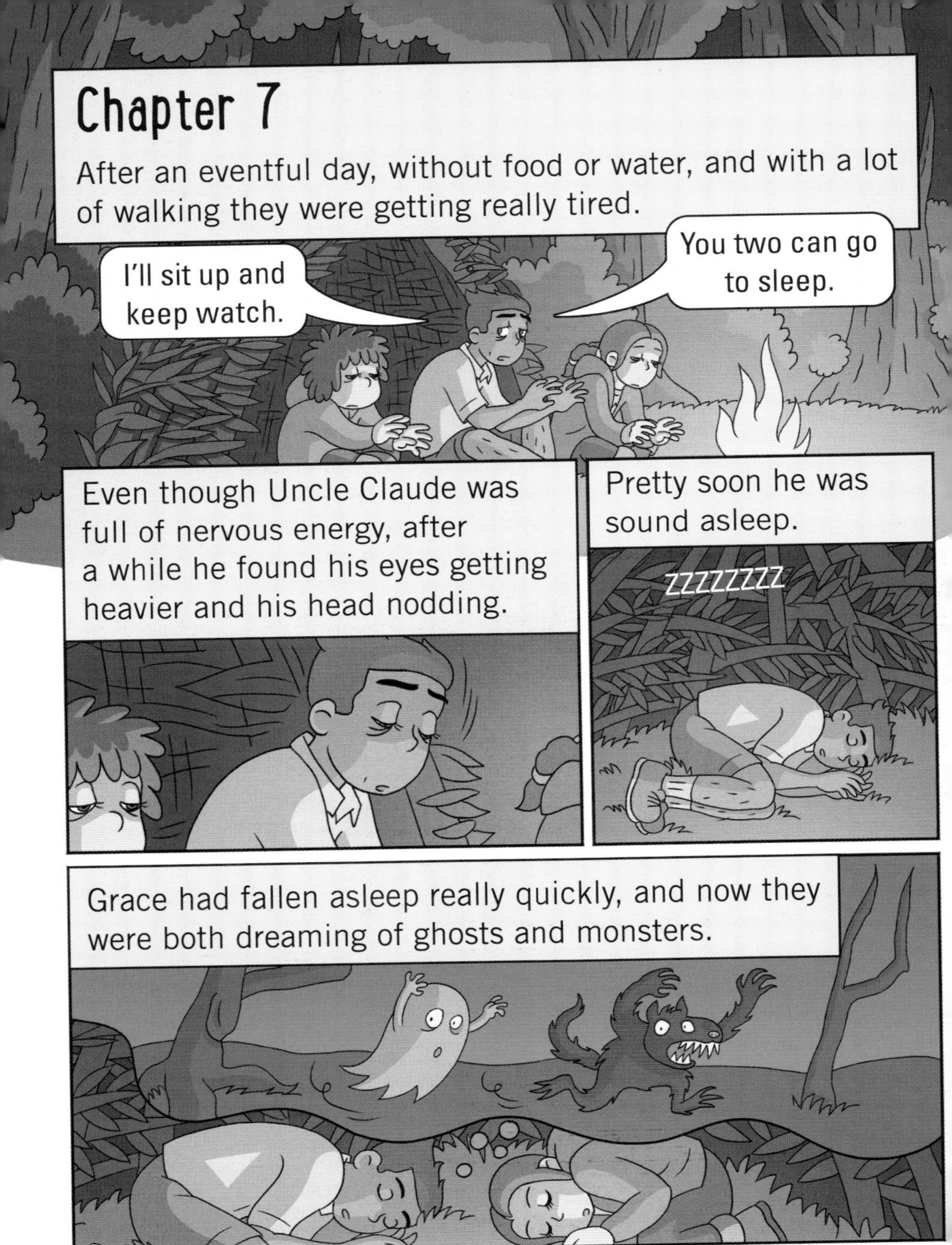
Chapter 7
After an eventful day, without food or water, and with a lot of walking they were getting really tired.
I'll sit up and keep watch.
You two can go to sleep.
Even though Uncle Claude was full of nervous energy, after a while he found his eyes getting heavier and his head nodding.
Pretty soon he was sound asleep.
ZZZZZZZZ
Grace had fallen asleep really quickly, and now they were both dreaming of ghosts and monsters.

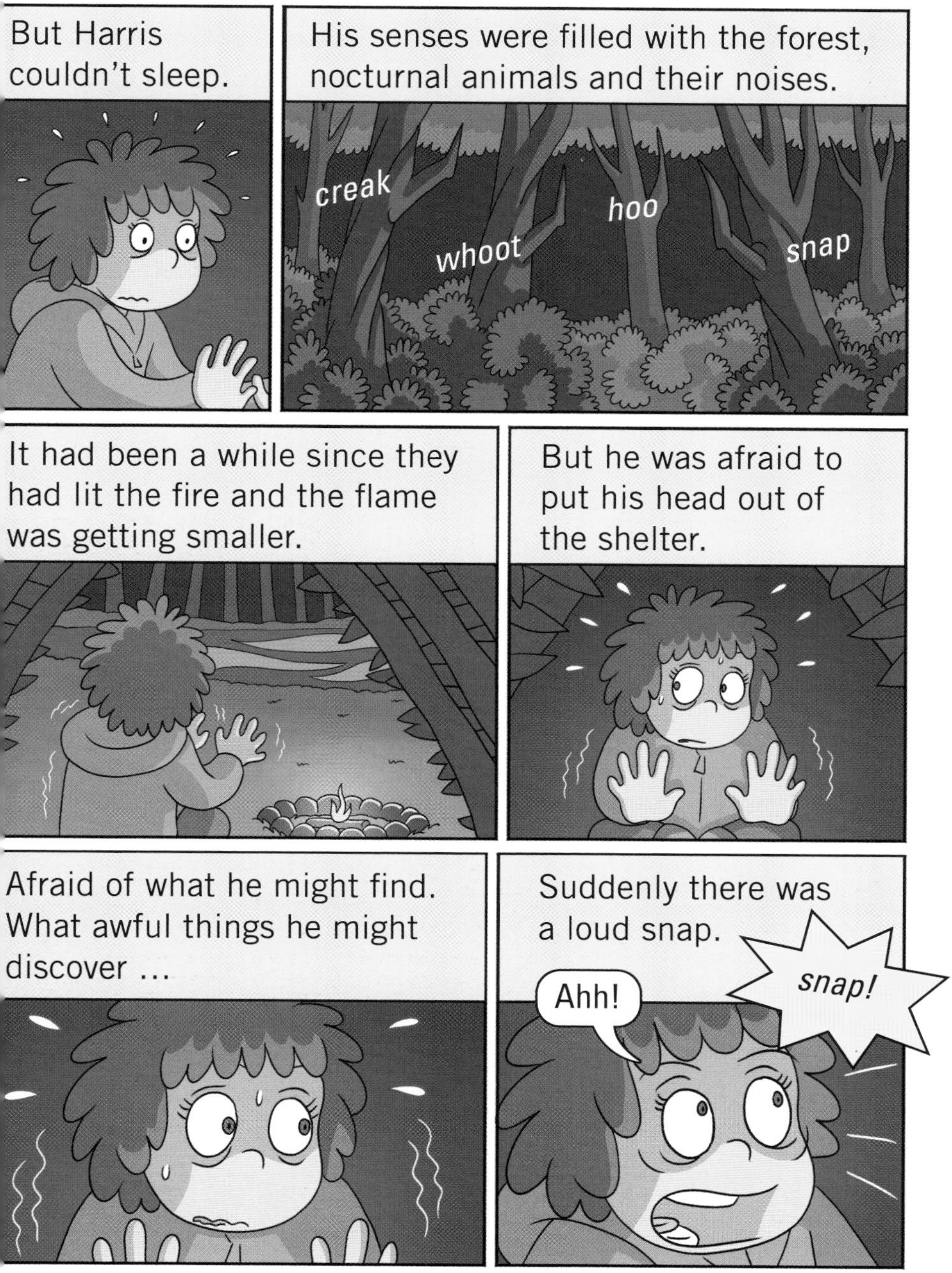
But Harris couldn't sleep.
His senses were filled with the forest, nocturnal animals and their noises.
creak
whoot
hoo
snap
It had been a while since they had lit the fire and the flame was getting smaller.
But he was afraid to put his head out of the shelter.
Afraid of what he might find. What awful things he might discover …
Suddenly there was a loud snap.
Ahh!
snap!

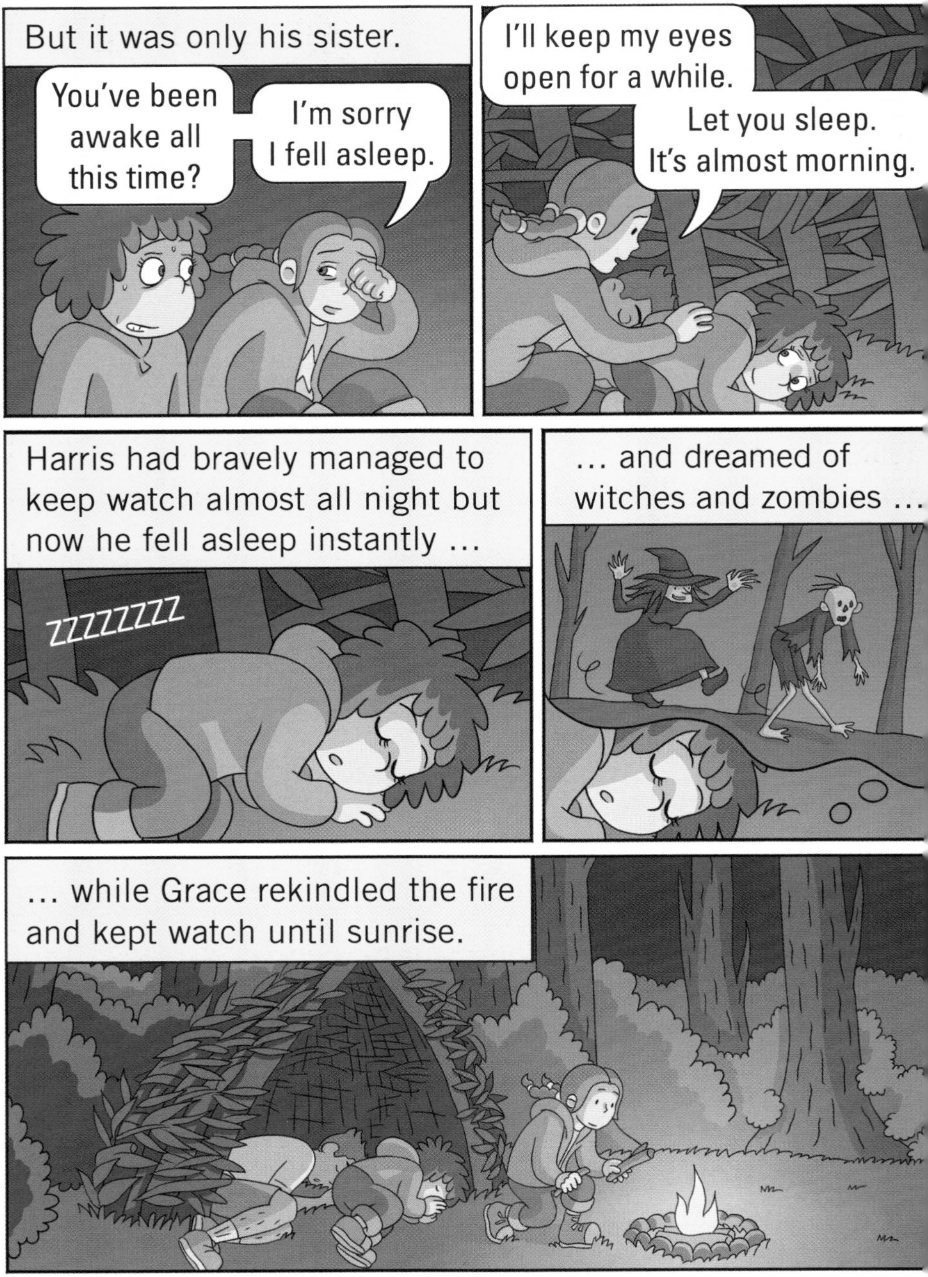
But it was only his sister.
You've been awake all this time?
I'm sorry I fell asleep.
I'll keep my eyes open for a while.
Let you sleep. It's almost morning.
Harris had bravely managed to keep watch almost all night but now he fell asleep instantly …
ZZZZZZZZ
… and dreamed of witches and zombies …
… while Grace rekindled the fire and kept watch until sunrise.

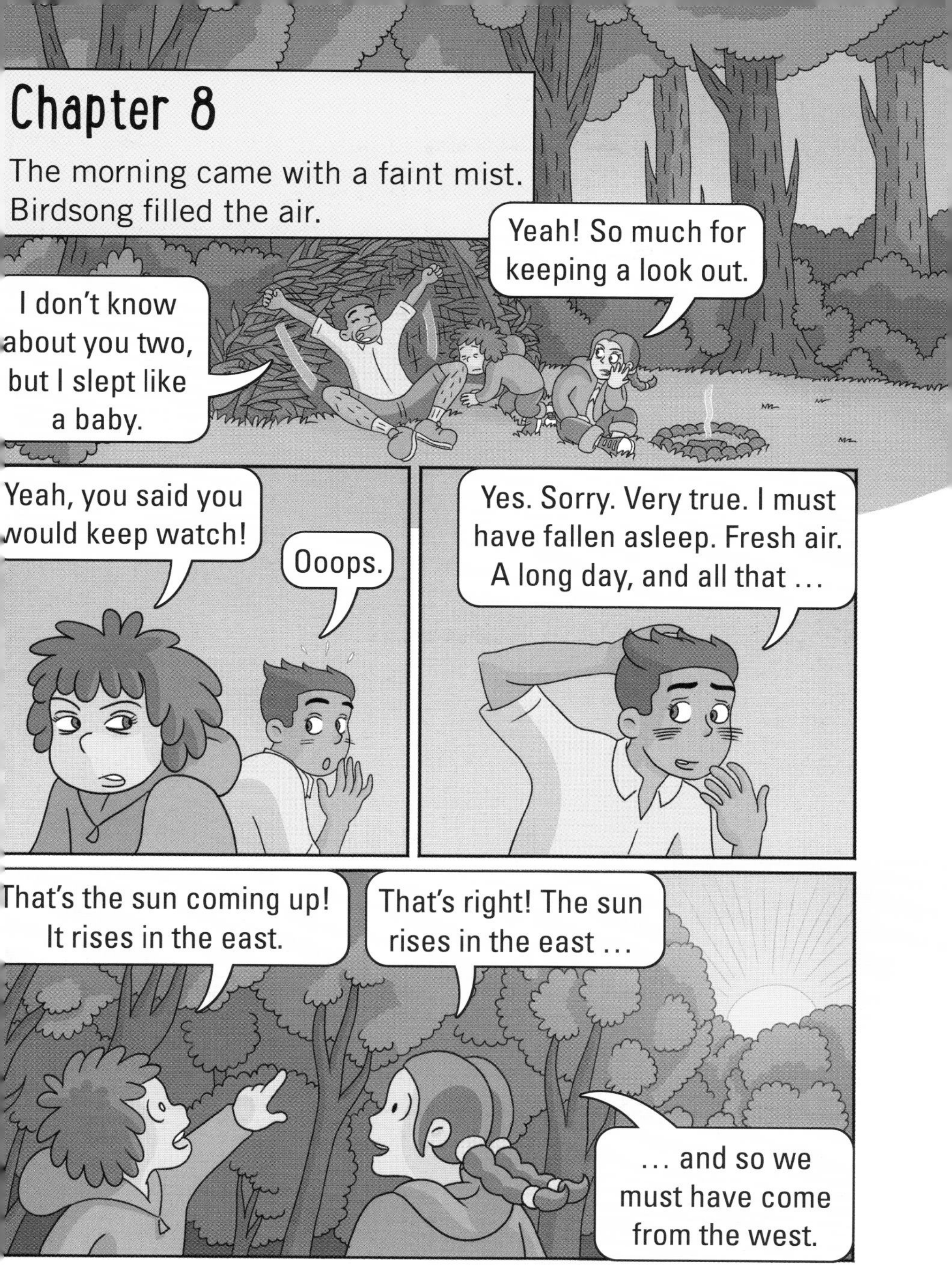
Chapter 8
The morning came with a faint mist. Birdsong filled the air.
I don't know about you two, but I slept like a baby.
Yeah! So much for keeping a look out.
Yeah, you said you would keep watch!
Ooops.
Yes. Sorry. Very true. I must have fallen asleep. Fresh air. A long day, and all that …
That's the sun coming up! It rises in the east.
That's right! The sun rises in the east …
… and so we must have come from the west.

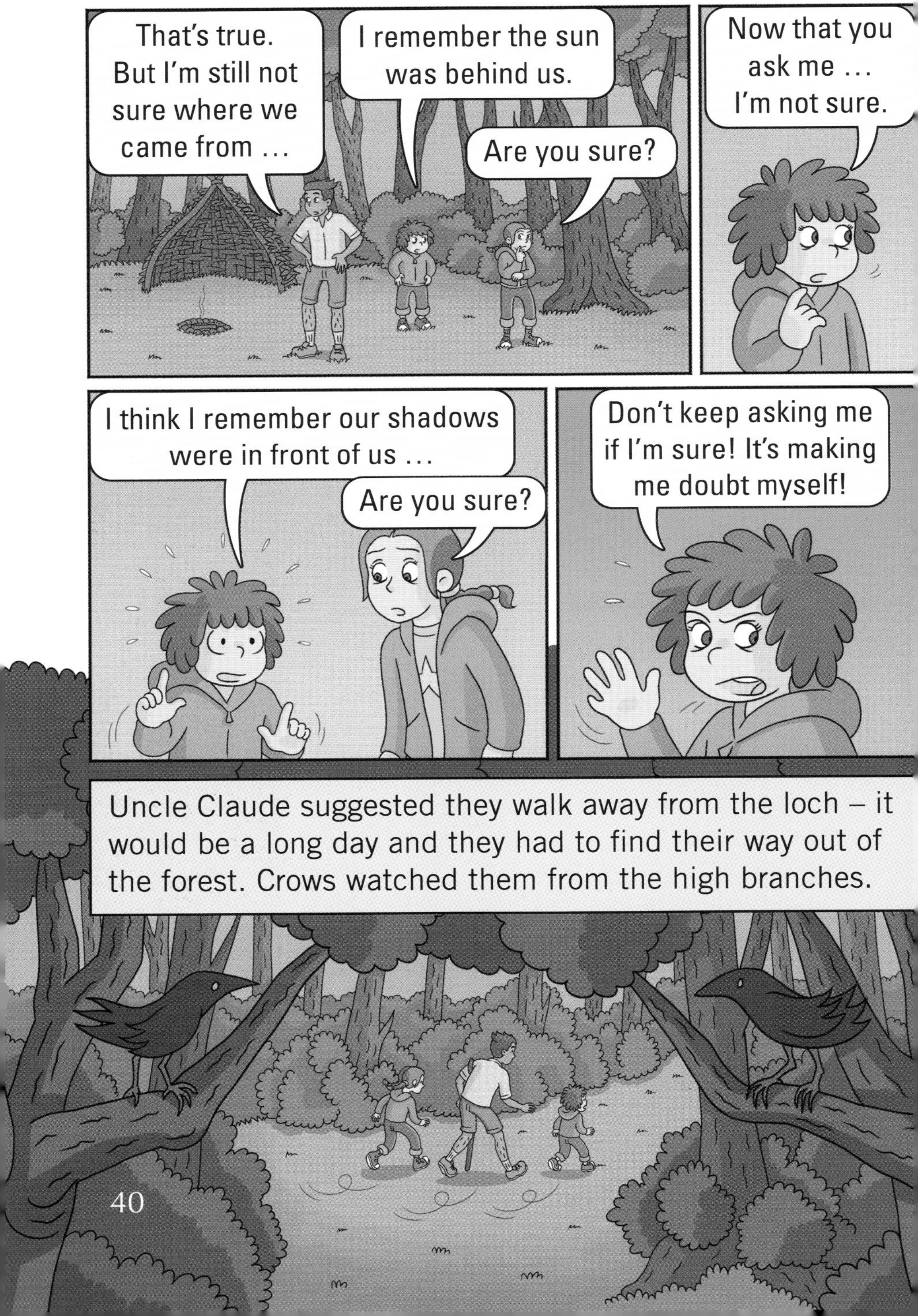
That's true. But I'm still not sure where we came from ...
I remember the sun was behind us.
Are you sure?
Now that you ask me ... I'm not sure.
I think I remember our shadows were in front of us ...
Are you sure?
Don't keep asking me if I'm sure! It's making me doubt myself!
Uncle Claude suggested they walk away from the loch – it would be a long day and they had to find their way out of the forest. Crows watched them from the high branches.

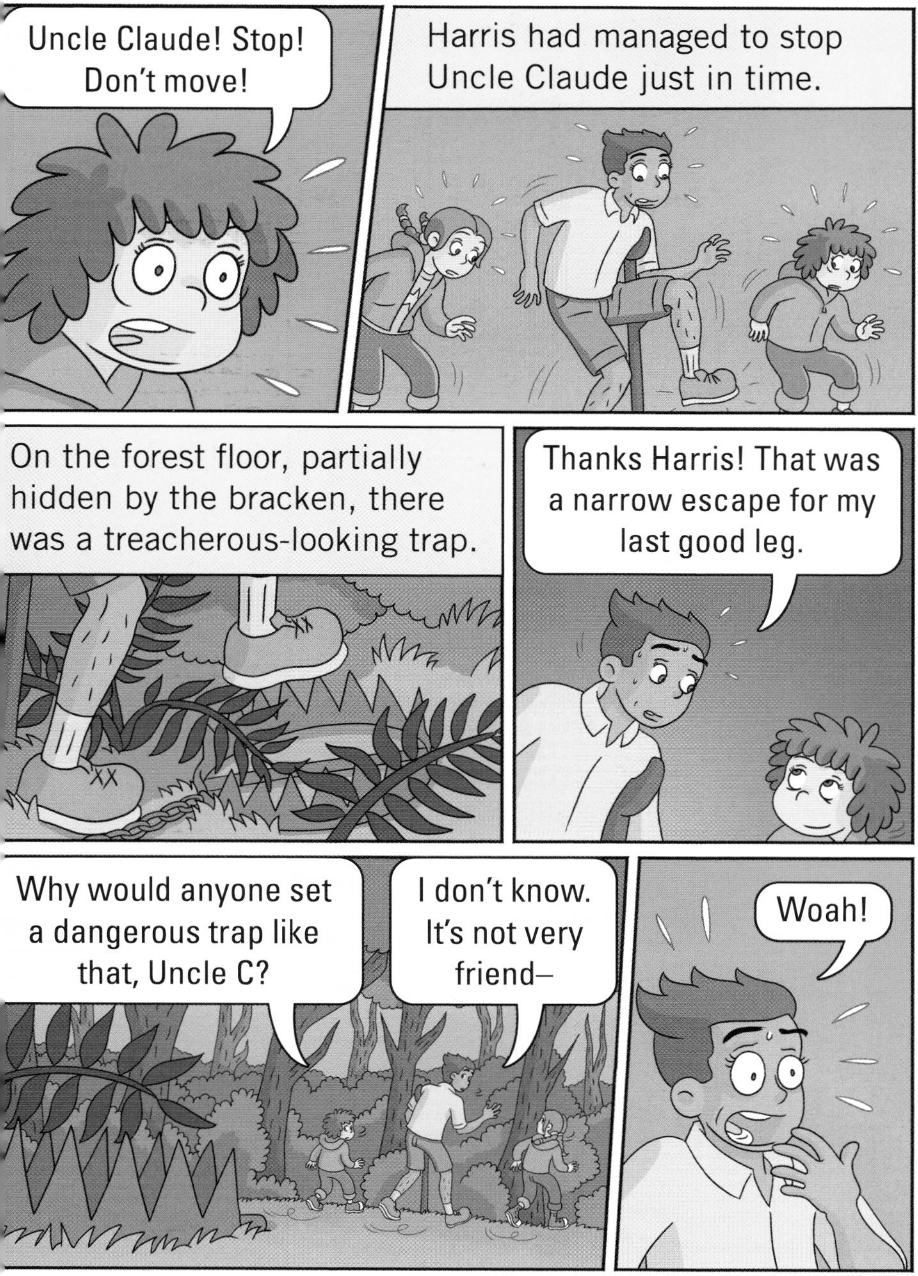
Uncle Claude! Stop!
Don't move!
Harris had managed to stop Uncle Claude just in time.
On the forest floor, partially hidden by the bracken, there was a treacherous-looking trap.
Thanks Harris! That was a narrow escape for my last good leg.
Why would anyone set a dangerous trap like that, Uncle C?
I don't know. It's not very friend–
Woah!

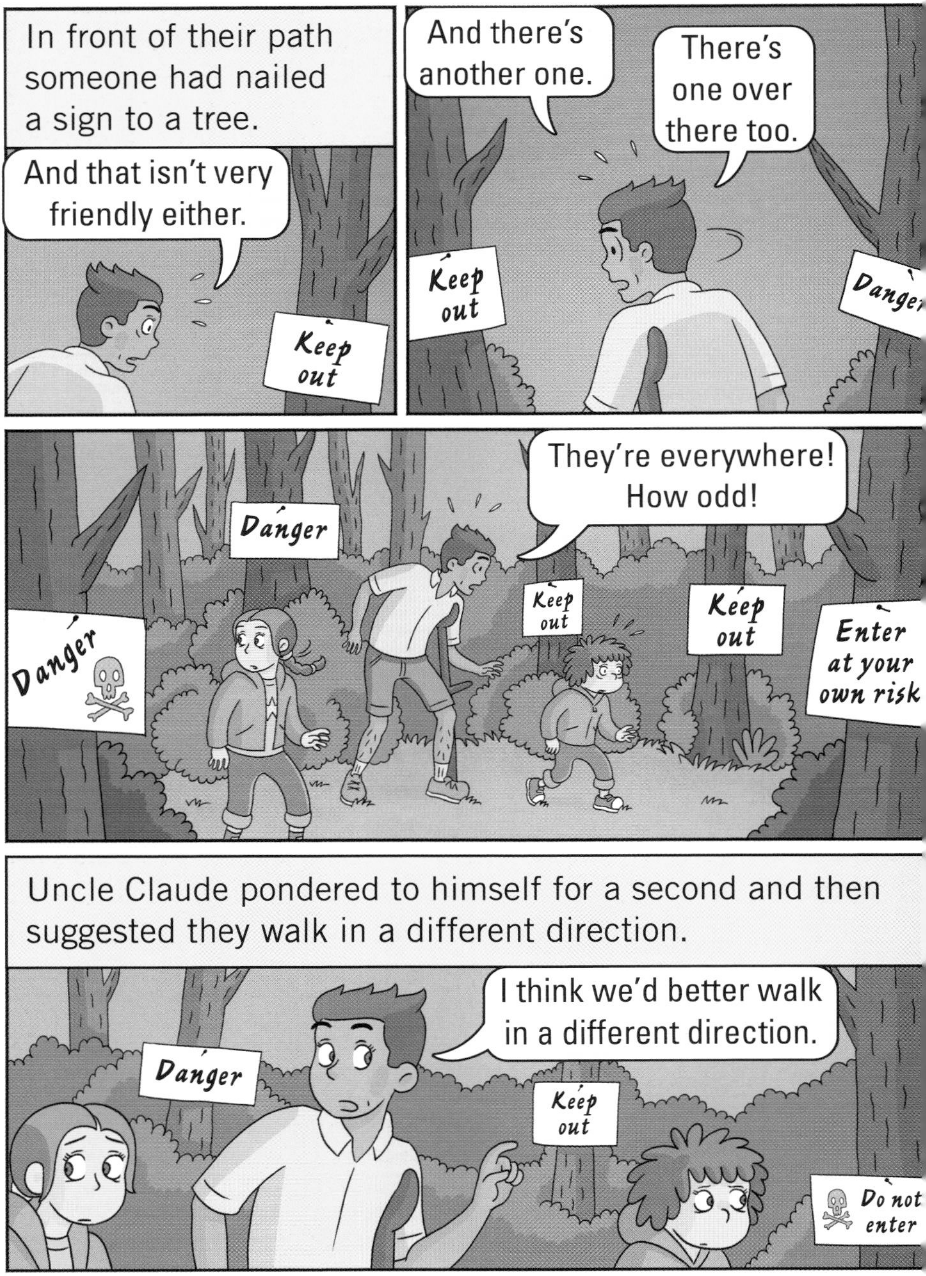
In front of their path someone had nailed a sign to a tree.
And that isn't very friendly either.
Keep out
And there's another one.
There's one over there too.
Keep out
They're everywhere! How odd!
Danger
Danger
Keep out
Keep out
Enter at your own risk
Uncle Claude pondered to himself for a second and then suggested they walk in a different direction.
I think we'd better walk in a different direction.
Danger
Keep out
Do not enter

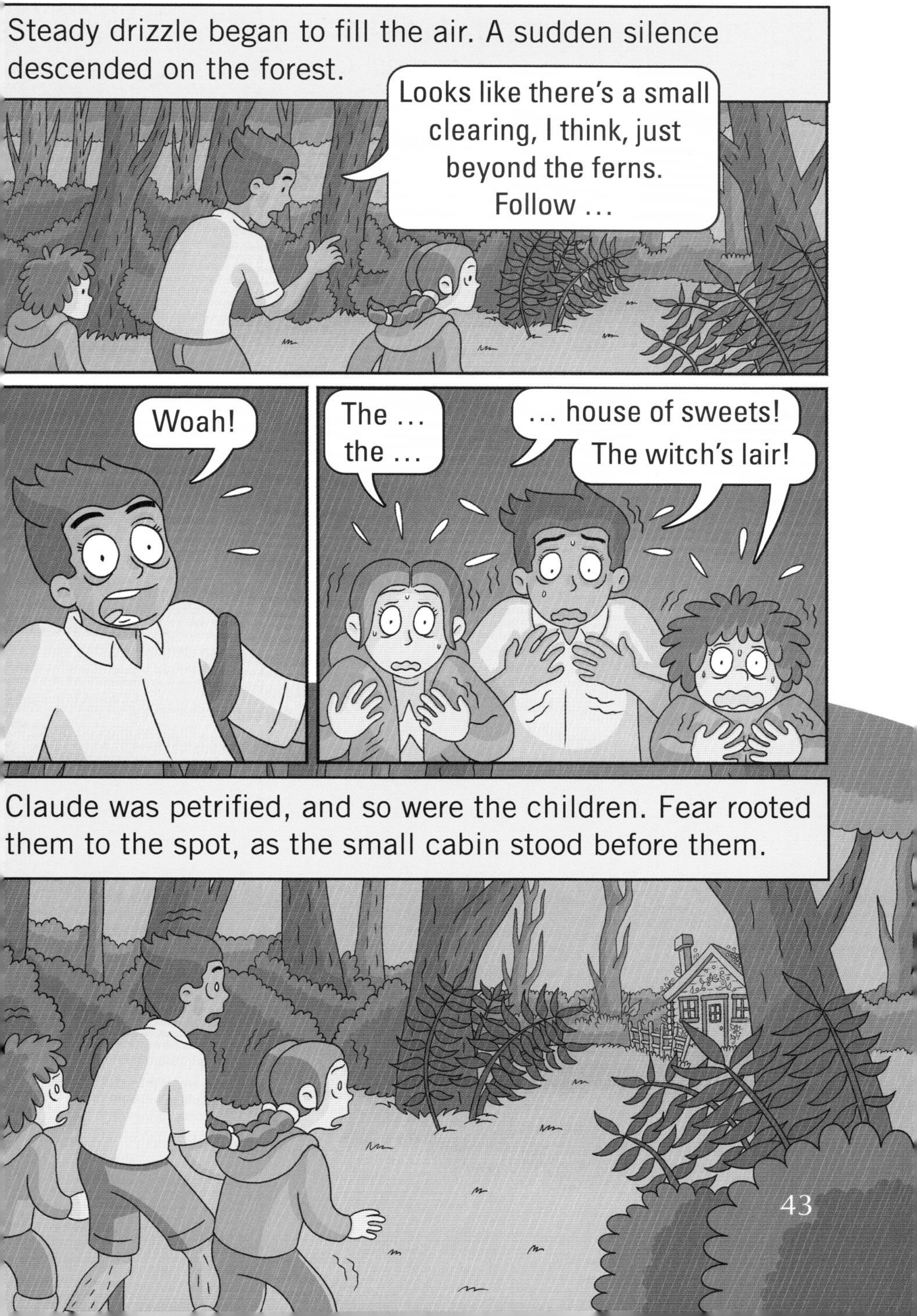
Steady drizzle began to fill the air. A sudden silence descended on the forest.
Looks like there's a small clearing, I think, just beyond the ferns. Follow …
Woah!
The … the …
… house of sweets!
The witch's lair!
Claude was petrified, and so were the children. Fear rooted them to the spot, as the small cabin stood before them.

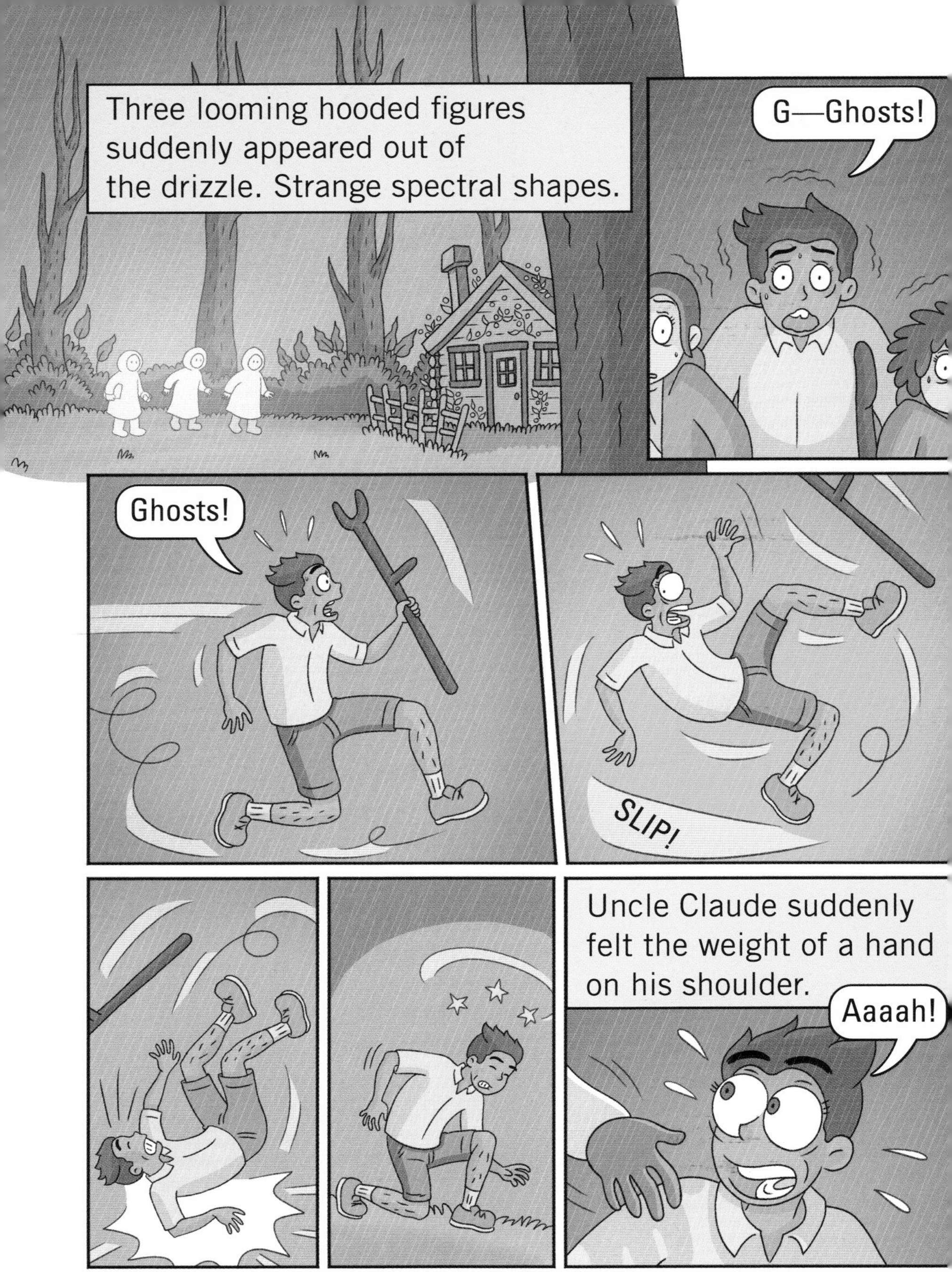
Three looming hooded figures suddenly appeared out of the drizzle. Strange spectral shapes.
G—Ghosts!
Ghosts!
SLIP!
Uncle Claude suddenly felt the weight of a hand on his shoulder.
Aaaah!

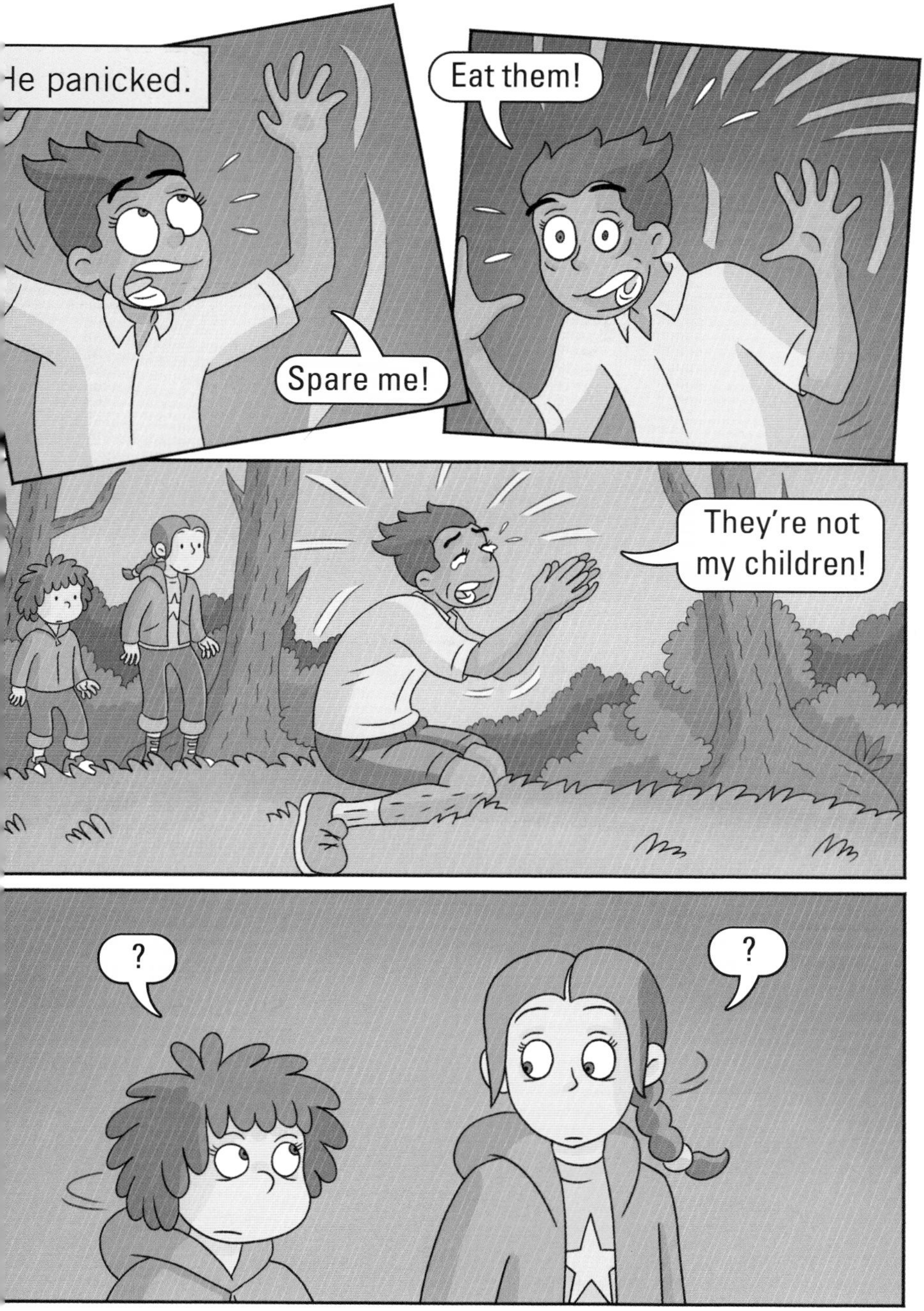

He panicked.
Spare me!
Eat them!
They're not my children!
?
?

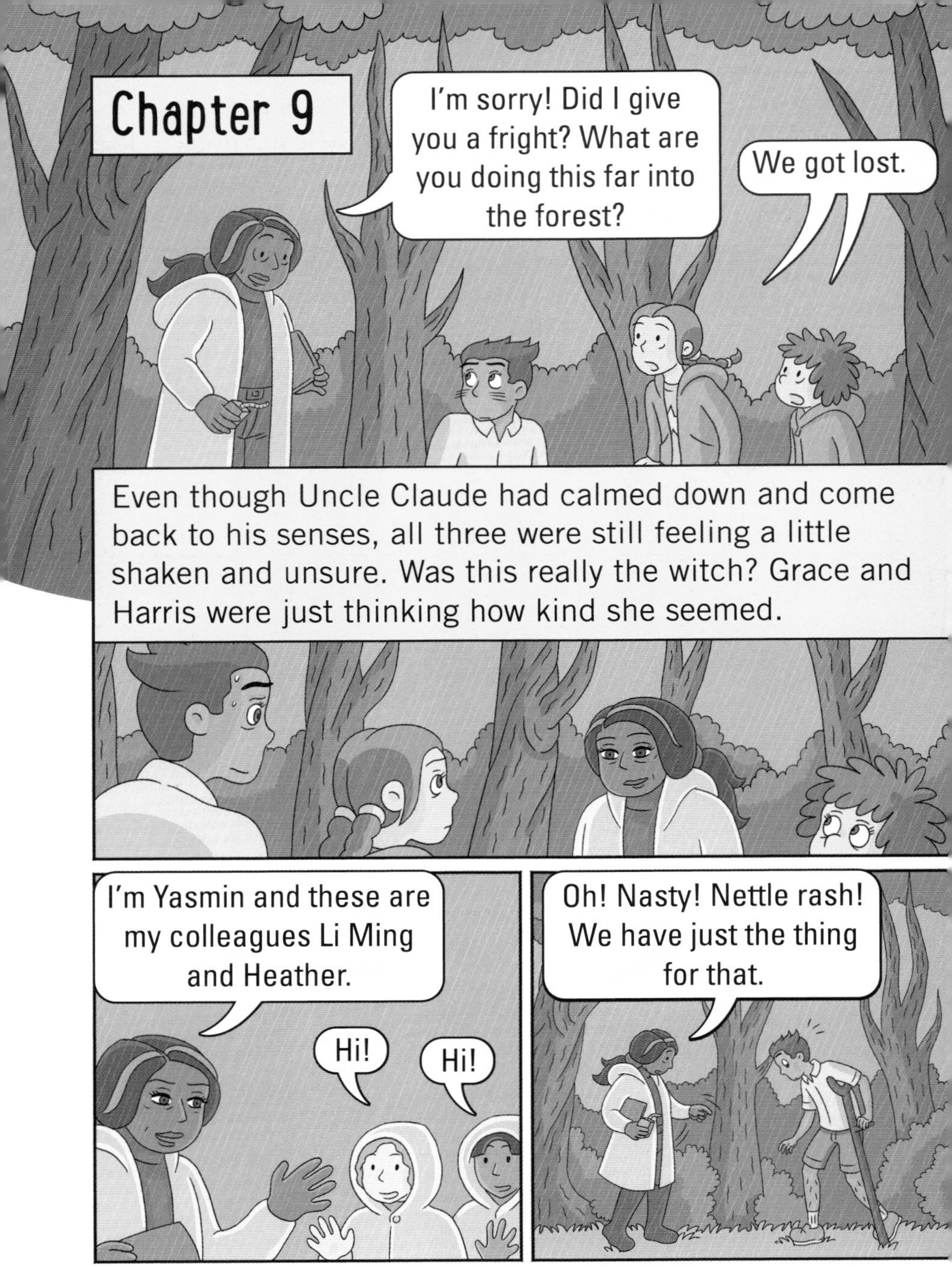
Chapter 9
I'm sorry! Did I give you a fright? What are you doing this far into the forest?
We got lost.
Even though Uncle Claude had calmed down and come back to his senses, all three were still feeling a little shaken and unsure. Was this really the witch? Grace and Harris were just thinking how kind she seemed.
I'm Yasmin and these are my colleagues Li Ming and Heather.
Hi!
Hi!
Oh! Nasty! Nettle rash! We have just the thing for that.

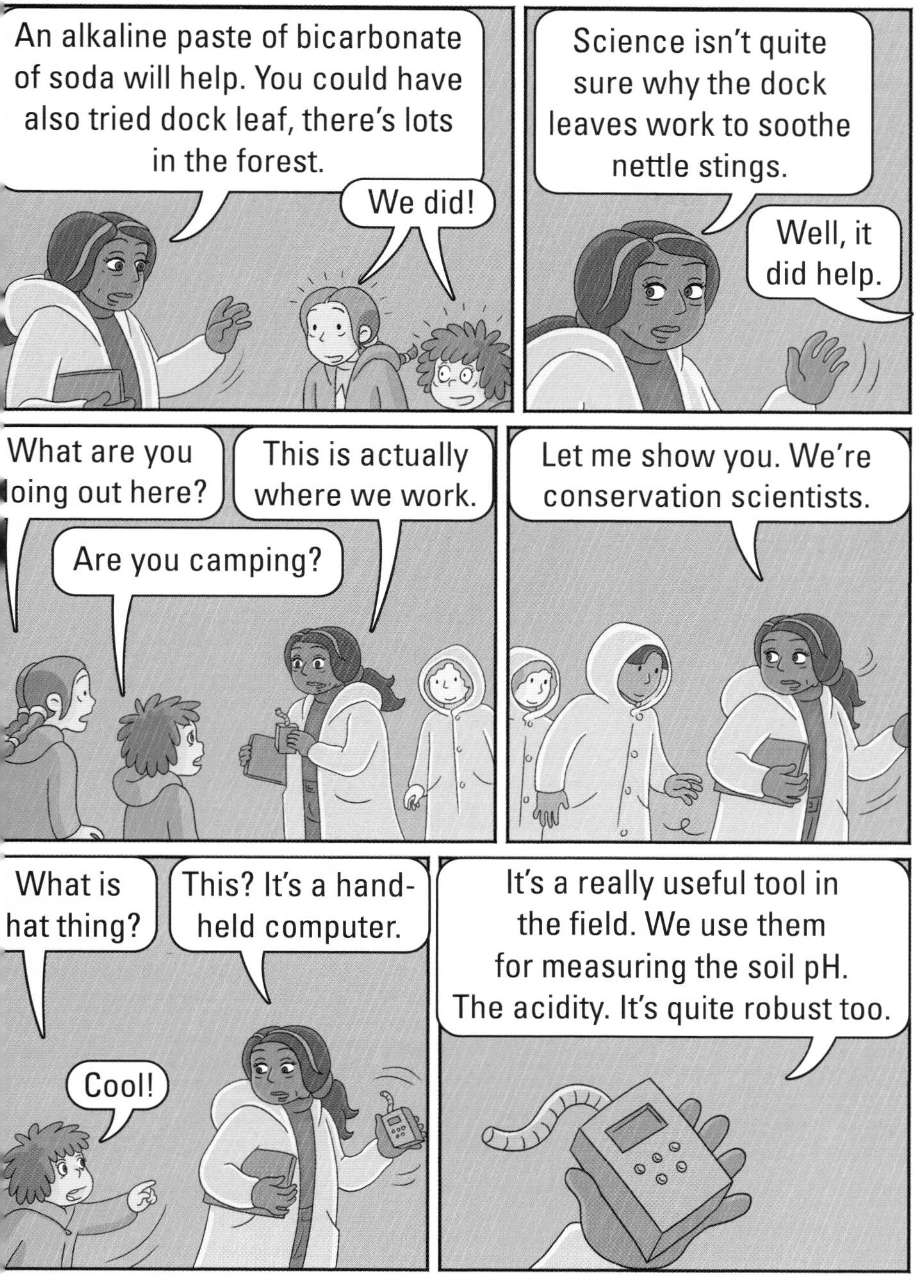
An alkaline paste of bicarbonate of soda will help. You could have also tried dock leaf, there's lots in the forest.
We did!
Science isn't quite sure why the dock leaves work to soothe nettle stings.
Well, it did help.
What are you loing out here?
This is actually where we work.
Are you camping?
Let me show you. We're conservation scientists.
What is hat thing?
This? It's a hand-held computer.
Cool!
It's a really useful tool in the field. We use them for measuring the soil pH. The acidity. It's quite robust too.

Uncle Claude and the children followed Yasmin. Up close they could see that the cabin was covered in pretty flowering climbing plants. Not sweets or cake.

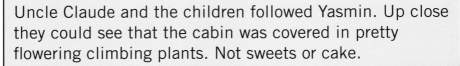

Inside, the house was full of herbs and other plants, and scientific equipment. It was warm and comforting after the cold, wet outdoors.

This is our base. We've been busy here for a couple of years now. It's important work. We need to know as much about our forests as we can.

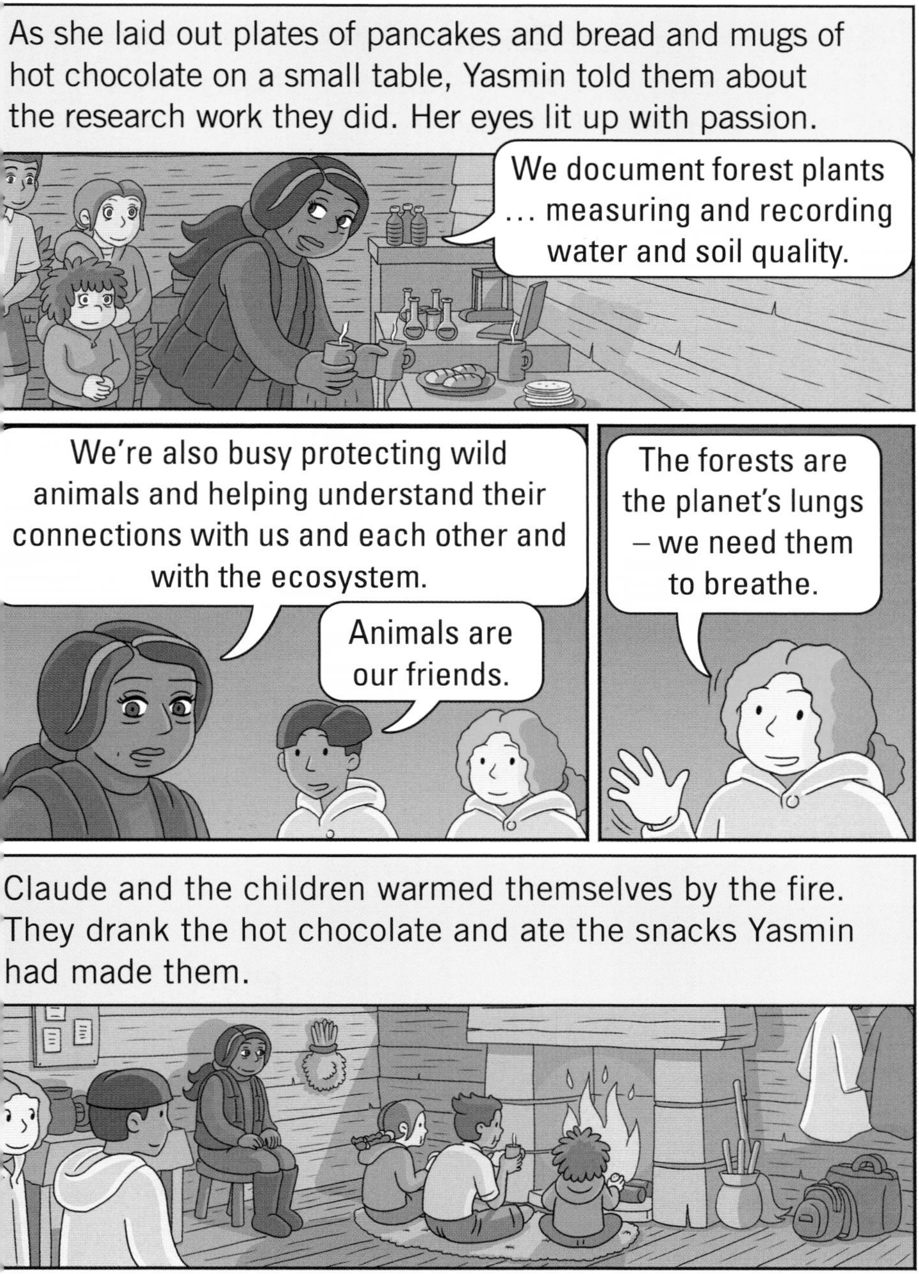
As she laid out plates of pancakes and bread and mugs of hot chocolate on a small table, Yasmin told them about the research work they did. Her eyes lit up with passion.
We document forest plants … measuring and recording water and soil quality.
We're also busy protecting wild animals and helping understand their connections with us and each other and with the ecosystem.
Animals are our friends.
The forests are the planet's lungs – we need them to breathe.
Claude and the children warmed themselves by the fire. They drank the hot chocolate and ate the snacks Yasmin had made them.

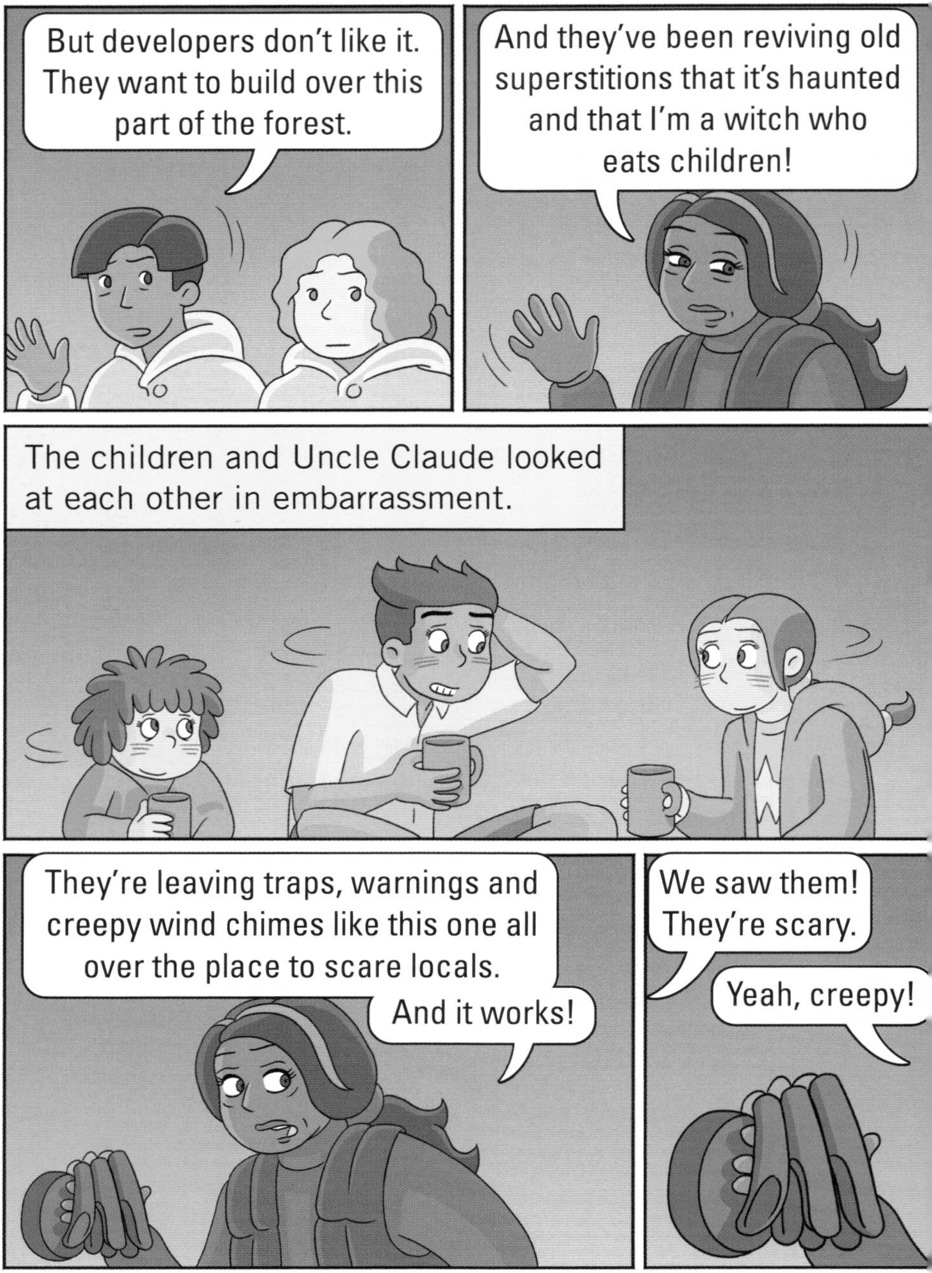

But developers don't like it. They want to build over this part of the forest.
And they've been reviving old superstitions that it's haunted and that I'm a witch who eats children!
The children and Uncle Claude looked at each other in embarrassment.
They're leaving traps, warnings and creepy wind chimes like this one all over the place to scare locals.
And it works!
We saw them! They're scary.
Yeah, creepy!

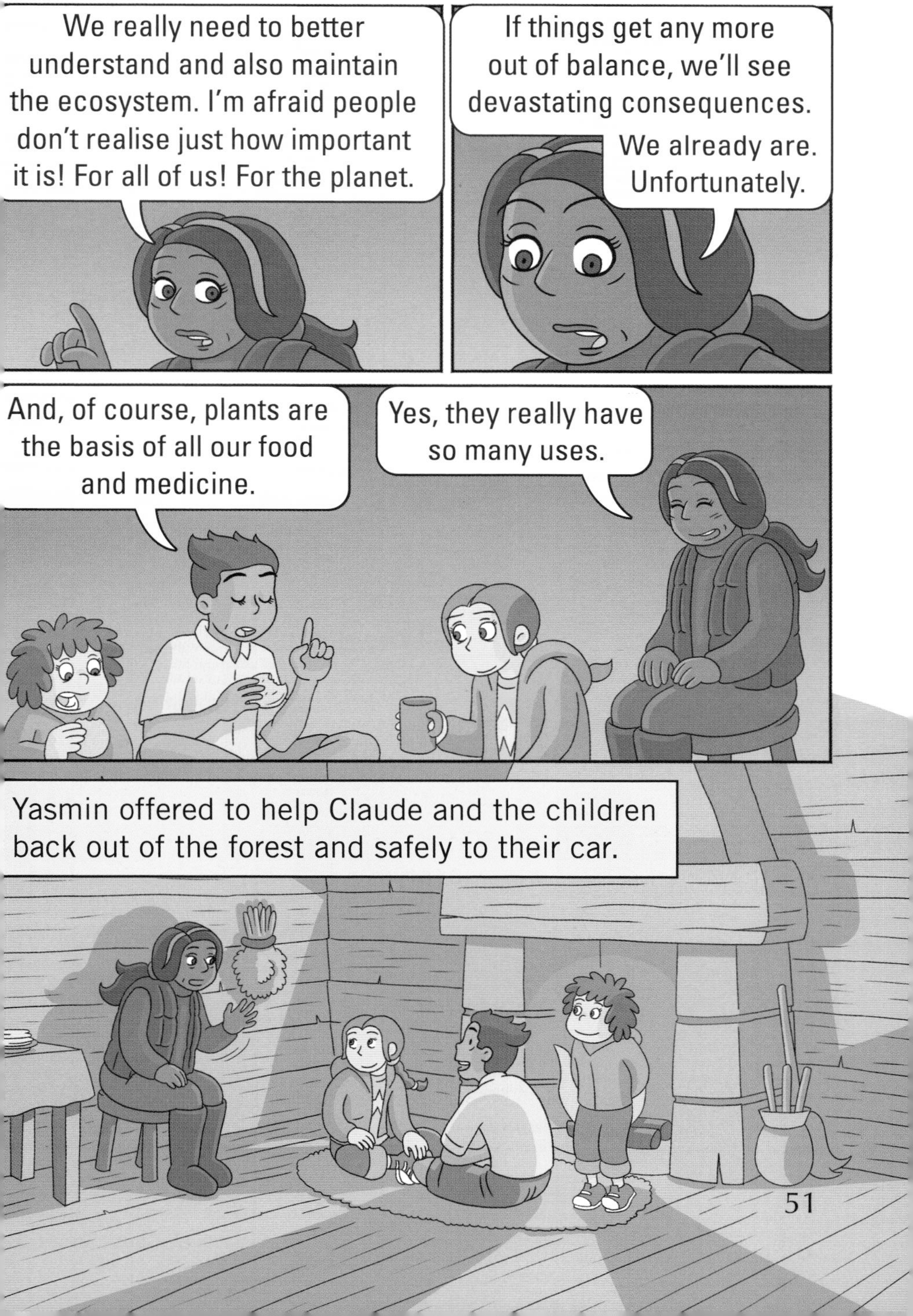
We really need to better understand and also maintain the ecosystem. I'm afraid people don't realise just how important it is! For all of us! For the planet.
If things get any more out of balance, we'll see devastating consequences.
We already are. Unfortunately.
And, of course, plants are the basis of all our food and medicine.
Yes, they really have so many uses.
Yasmin offered to help Claude and the children back out of the forest and safely to their car.

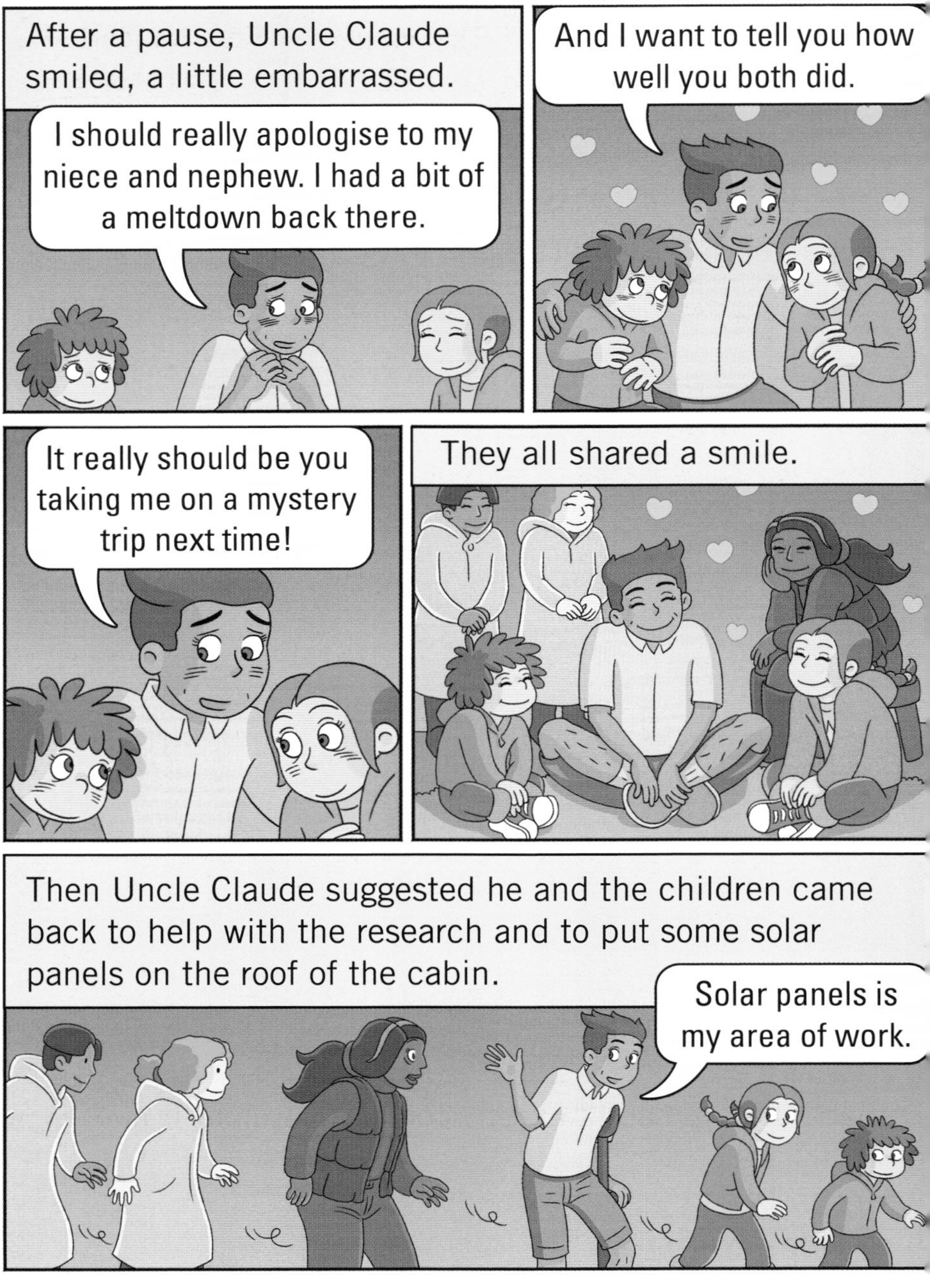
After a pause, Uncle Claude smiled, a little embarrassed.
I should really apologise to my niece and nephew. I had a bit of a meltdown back there.
And I want to tell you how well you both did.
It really should be you taking me on a mystery trip next time!
They all shared a smile.
Then Uncle Claude suggested he and the children came back to help with the research and to put some solar panels on the roof of the cabin.
Solar panels is my area of work.

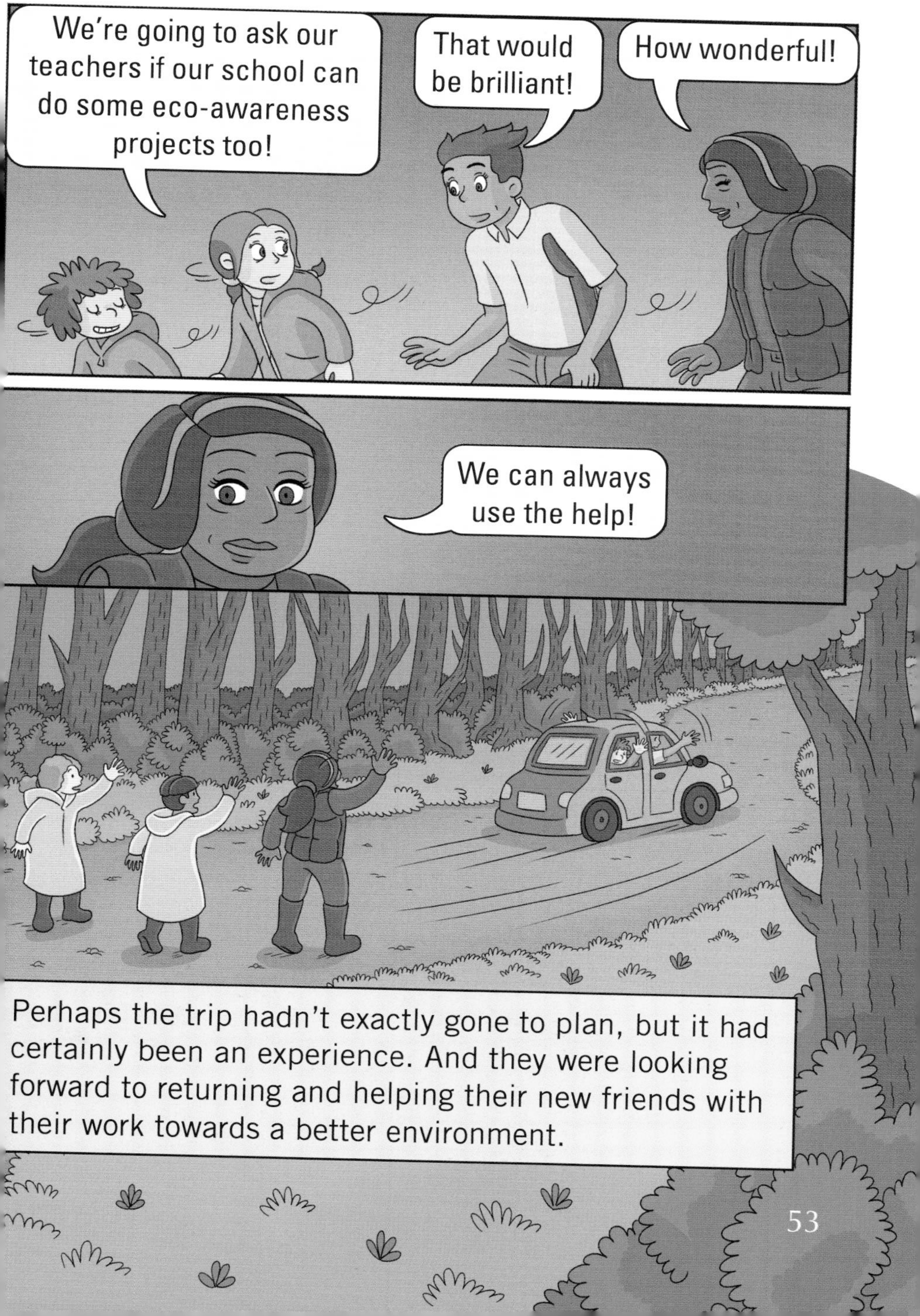
We're going to ask our teachers if our school can do some eco-awareness projects too!
That would be brilliant!
How wonderful!
We can always use the help!
Perhaps the trip hadn't exactly gone to plan, but it had certainly been an experience. And they were looking forward to returning and helping their new friends with their work towards a better environment.

Harris and Grace emotion journey

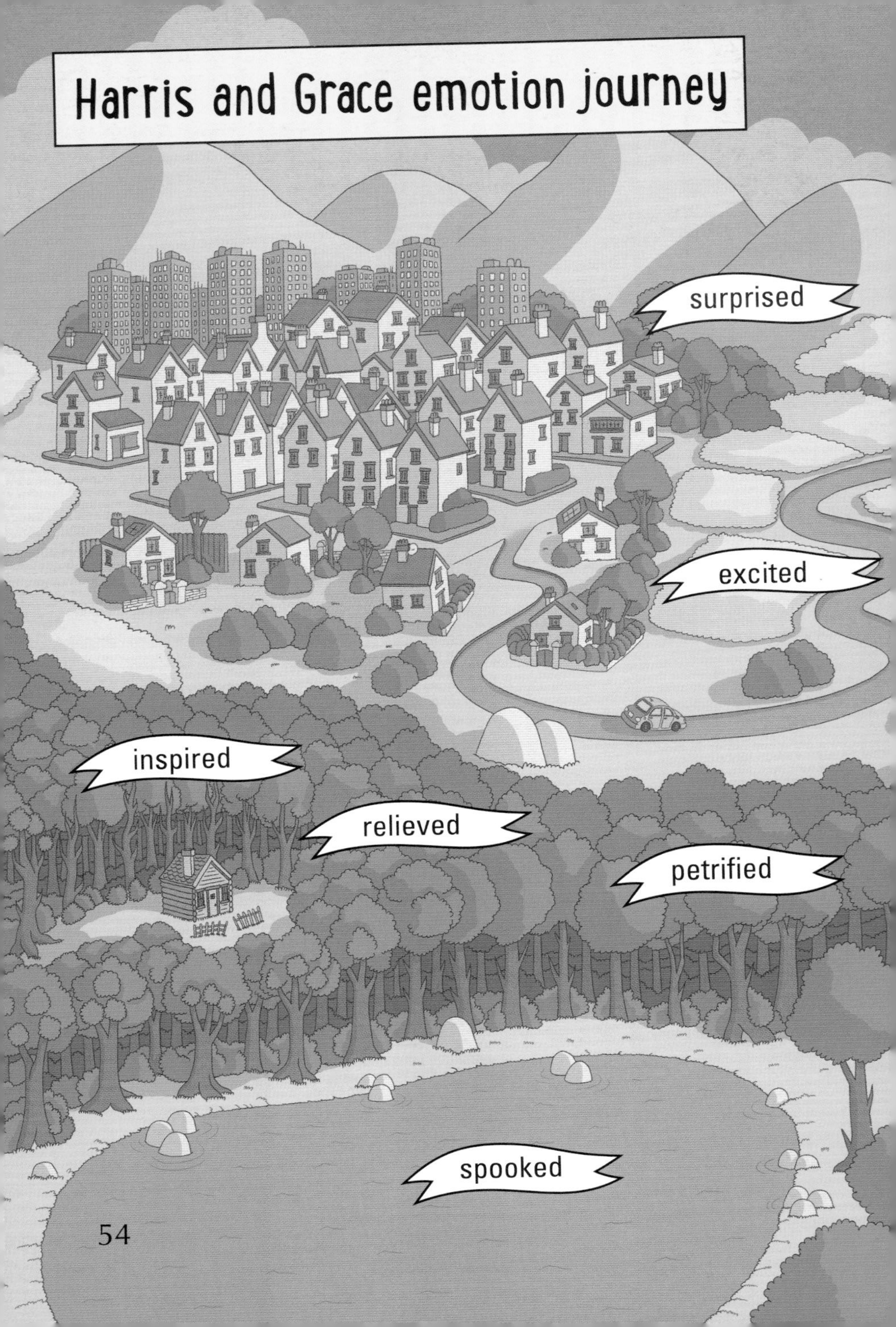
surprised
excited
inspired
relieved
petrified
spooked